ARMADA

BY STRENGTH AND GUILE - BOOK 2

PAUL TEAGUE
JON EVANS

IMAGINARY BROTHER

PROLOGUE

"We're almost in firing range, Admiral," said Commander Vernon. The bridge of *Vengeance* was quiet as the two ships played cat and mouse.

"What are they doing this far out in space?" murmured Stansfield, frowning as he watched the Astute19 Class battleship *Centurion* on his screen. "There's nowhere to go, nowhere to hide. They must have known that we would catch them eventually."

"Ready to launch torpedoes, Admiral," said Midshipman Henry at the weapons console.

"Hold steady, Mr Henry," said Stansfield. "Mr Khan, let's see if we can hail them."

"Opening a channel now, sir." Midshipman Khan gave Stansfield a nod.

"*Vengeance* to *Centurion*, this is Admiral Thomas Stansfield. You are to heave to immediately and prepare to be boarded, or we will be forced to open fire."

"Nothing, sir," said Khan.

"*Vengeance* to *Centurion*, heave to, prepare to be boarded."

"They've opened their aft torpedo ports, sir, and their scanners are active. No other response."

"Prepare to fire, Mr Henry, and switch our defensive systems to fully automatic," said Stansfield, his tone calm and dark, "but let's give them a little longer to respond."

"They've no intention of talking, sir," said Vernon, interrupting the silence. His face glistened with sweat.

"Agreed, but let's just give them one more opportunity to climb down. We're both in Astute19 Class battleships. They must know that we out-skill them, that they haven't got a chance."

"Damned terrorists! I can't believe they managed to pull it off in the first place," said Lieutenant Yau.

"What makes you so sure they're terrorists?" said Stansfield quietly. "One more try, please, Mr Khan."

Then a warning siren sounded.

"Incoming, sir, two Nightshade torpedoes locked on, impact in one minute and counting."

"Defensive fire, Mr Henry. Forward railgun batteries, clear the path."

Vengeance rattled as the forward batteries opened fire on the incoming torpedoes.

"Fifteen seconds," said Henry, throwing a timer onto the main display. The bridge was silent as they watched the torpedoes approach, picked out in green so that they were visible against the stars. Then they both flared like short-lived stars as the railgun rounds tore through them.

"Torpedoes destroyed, sir," said Henry unnecessarily.

"Thank you, Mr Henry," said Stansfield drily. "Re-open the channel. We'll give this one more try, then we go in." Stansfield opened a new channel. "Are your teams ready, Lieutenant Commander Grant?"

Grant's voice came over the speaker. "Ay, sir. Raptor teams primed and ready to fly."

Stansfield nodded and switched channels.

"*Vengeance* to *Centurion*, last chance. Heave to and prepare to be boarded. Your unprovoked attack will not go unpunished. We will open fire if–"

"Incoming, sir. Four more torpedoes heading our way." Henry's tone was urgent now.

Stansfield swore under his breath, but the time for politeness had passed.

"Defensive fire," he ordered. "Raptors, launch as soon as the ship steadies, torpedoes to target the helm and engine, I want her disabled, not destroyed."

The four torpedoes exploded harmlessly, ripped apart by railgun rounds while they were still kilometres clear of *Vengeance*.

"Raptors launching, sir," said Grant.

"Fire torpedoes, Mr Henry. Two-four-two configuration: let's play them at their own game and take her down." Stansfield was ready for the fight now, and he didn't plan to lose.

Down in the bays, Raptor assault teams launched into space, the Eagle Nebula providing a spectacular backdrop to the battle.

In groups of eight, the Raptors moved swiftly into assault clusters, weapons ready to wear down *Centurion's* defensive capabilities.

"Why *Centurion*, Ed?" Stansfield asked Vernon, as they monitored the assault on the command consoles. "That has to be significant, doesn't it? And the timing?"

"You may be reading too much into it," said Vernon as the first volley of torpedoes left *Vengeance's* turrets. "*Centurion* was in *Kingdom 10* for repairs, it was closest and easiest to attack in this part of space."

Kingdom 10 was a naval staging post, an orbital base designed to construct and support deep space operations.

"But do you think it's her? Has she come back for his ship?"

"Incoming," said Henry. "Sustained fire this time, they're not letting up."

"Continue railgun fire," said Stansfield, frowning as he tried to work out what *Centurion* was doing. "Raptors to intercept."

A cluster of eight Raptors separated from the main assault group to target the incoming weapons. Stansfield and Vernon watched the battle unfold over tens of kilometres of space as the two ships battered at each other.

"Brace for impact," warned Henry suddenly, fear edging his voice.

The explosions came immediately, and *Vengeance* shook. The lighting flickered, and damage and casualty reports began to flow into the bridge from elsewhere on the ship.

"We have damage to crew quarters," said Vernon, "and casualties in engineering."

"They came out of nowhere," said Stansfield, frowning at the screen as he tried to work out what had happened. "What happened, Grant? Where did those torpedoes come from?" Stansfield had been caught off-guard, and he was rattled by how little warning they'd had before the impact.

"Grant's dead," came a voice Stansfield didn't know. "Heavy damage in the bays, at least nine dead down here."

"Goddammit," Vernon cursed under his breath.

"Ten degrees down and a sixty-second burn on the main engines," ordered Stansfield. "Let's give these people a run for their money. Fire again. I want her disabled, Mr Henry, not destroyed."

"Ay, sir,"

"Sustained torpedo fire targeting the engines. Raptors, I want as much superficial damage as possible, but do not – repeat – do *not* take out the core."

The Raptors moved in, and Stansfield knew that *Centurion* didn't have the crew to return the favour. Their adversary had only the big guns and torpedoes and that was bad enough, even though it gave *Vengeance* the advantage.

The Raptors were closing fast, firing mid-calibre railgun rounds and short-range needle missiles. *Centurion*'s hull flared as the missiles blasted her armour, sending fragments of debris floating off to join the stars.

Torpedoes struck both *Centurion* and *Vengeance* as the two vast battleships traded blows. *Vengeance* shook under the pounding.

"We have them on the run," said Vernon, sensing an early and easy victory.

"Don't hold your breath," muttered Stansfield, a worried frown on his face. "There's not many organisations could pull off something of this scale."

"Something's happening ahead, Admiral." Lieutenant Yau, the science officer, was examining his screen, trying to figure out what he was looking at.

"Details, Lieutenant," said Vernon.

"It's the anomaly again, Commander. Scanning now to confirm."

"Let's get as much information about this thing as we can," said Stansfield, leaning forward in his command chair. "I want full scans, everything we have. I need to know the size, source, purpose and origins."

Stansfield surveyed the bridge to ensure his team were moving fast on his request. The ship shook again as another torpedo struck the hull, and several of the bridge crew were thrown to the floor.

"This is the best chance we're going to get to take a good look at this thing. Sol's detected it only five times before; we *need* this data."

"The anomaly is increasing in size, sir, and *Centurion* is heading straight for it," said Yau.

"They're going to go *through* it?" said Vernon incredulously. "We need to see what that thing is."

"Agreed. Helm, put us on a course to hit the anomaly, and fire main engines. Match their speed, we're going in after them," Stansfield ordered.

"The anomaly is still increasing in size, Admiral," said Lieutenant Yau.

"If I didn't know better, Lieutenant, I'd say it was a wormhole, wouldn't you?"

"Too soon to say, sir. I'm scouring the databases, but we have nothing on record of this size and nature. Whoever – or whatever – created it, it's not one of ours."

The screen at the front of the bridge was now zoomed in on the colourful array ahead of them. It looked like a fissure in space, a swirling mass of colour, and weirdly disorienting against the glittering darkness of the stars.

It was a spectacular sight, and it had appeared out of nowhere, deep in space, light years from anything of significance to Sol. Only the *Kingdom 10* outpost was located close by, everyone having long decided that this part of space held no particular interest.

"Sixty seconds until *Centurion* passes through the anomaly," reported Yau.

"But the question is, what does it do? Is it a force field? A wormhole of some sort? An unmasked singularity? A giant TV screen?"

"It could have a defensive purpose," said Vernon. "Maybe we should pull back the Raptors?"

Vernon waited for Stansfield's response. The anomaly looked beautiful from afar, but they had no way to know if it was benign.

"Agreed. Commander, pull them back to ten kilometres. We're not going to stop *Centurion* now, so we'll let them pass through and follow if it looks like it's safe to proceed."

Vernon passed orders to the Raptors as Stansfield studied the images they were returning to *Vengeance*.

"*Centurion* entering now, sir," came Yau's update. "It seems benign."

The bridge crew watched in awe as *Centurion* passed through the coloured vortex. Now *Vengeance*'s torpedoes were exploding before reaching their target, and *Centurion* was left unharmed.

"We're following them," said Stansfield, making a snap decision. "Helm, increase speed. Vernon, get the Raptors to follow; we'll resume the assault once we're through."

"I'd recommend caution, Admiral," said Vernon quietly as he updated the Raptors' orders. "We don't know what's on the other side. There could be anything waiting for us in there."

"Your concern is noted, Ed," said Stansfield. "But you know why we have to go through. If she's on the other side of that thing, we have to finish this. It has to end here."

Vernon and Stansfield looked at each other for a few seconds before the commander nodded. Stansfield was right. There was no other way.

"The anomaly is closing, sir," said Yau. "It's going to be too small for us by the time we reach it."

"Fire the engines, maximum power," said Stansfield. "I do *not* want to lose them."

"Admiral," Vernon protested. "We're not going to make it, we need to pull back!"

Vengeance's engines roared and the battleship shot forwards, charging toward the anomaly even as it shrank before their eyes.

But as they reached the spot where *Centurion* had vanished into the portal, all that remained was the empty blackness of space.

1

The bridge of *Vengeance* was completely silent. Slowly, the crew returned to their posts, watching the metal forms of the Mechs like hawks to be certain that they were now disabled.

"Let's have your reports, please!" said Stansfield, his voice booming across the bridge. "Are you fit to continue, Lieutenant Yau?" The Lieutenant had picked up a light wound during the fighting, and one side of his head was now covered in spray-on artificial skin.

"Yes, Admiral, it's only superficial, I'll carry on until relief can be found. The medbay have more important things to deal with."

They had survived the Mechs' assault. It wasn't the first time they'd fought an unknown enemy in this part of space, but Stansfield couldn't recall any action so desperate.

"Are you sure those Mechs are safe?" Vernon asked, walking up to one, his weapon still at the ready, prodding its limp form with his foot.

"We have fatalities across the ship, Admiral," said Midshipman Khan, reading off his screen. "Between forty and seventy, with at least as many wounded or unaccounted for."

"No major structural damage," said Yau as he peered at the integrity monitors, "but there are several hull breaches created by the

Mechs to gain entry, elevators are out all over, lots of internal damage from the fighting. No fires. It's going to be some repair job."

"Davies, how certain are you that the Mechs are dead?" Stansfield asked.

"Not sure, sir. Do you want an honest answer or an optimistic answer?"

Stansfield wasn't in the mood for bullshit. "Just give me a damned answer!" he snapped. "How likely are these things to suddenly jump up and start shooting at us again?"

"I don't know, sir," admitted Davies. "I worked out how to disrupt power and take out a core area of these panels, but this tech is completely unfamiliar to me. I mean, it has buttons, lights, switches and interfaces–only, this is nothing like I've ever seen in Sol."

"Keep working. If there's any sign of these creatures being re-activated, scream." He closed the channel and turned to Commander Vernon. "Clear the bridge of all Mechs. Dump the corpses into space. Then prioritise Level One, the bays and the med areas."

"Ay, sir," said Vernon, already moving.

"Where's Woodhall?" said Stansfield, looking around the bridge. Nobody seemed to know. "Find him and get him down to the workshop to assist Fernandez." Stansfield exchanged a glance with Vernon. "Corporal Conway, report."

"Are you seeing this, Admiral? It's so far off I can't even begin to make it out with our onboard kit. Can *Vengeance* do any better?"

"Negative. We're blind at the moment, we've sustained serious systems damage. Mr Khan, do we still have comms with Sol?"

"Yes and no, sir." Stansfield glared at the midshipman. "The comms line is still open, sir, but the signal from Sol is seriously degraded, even though they seem to receive our data."

"Explanation?"

"I don't have one, sir," said Khan.

"Davies. Your thoughts?"

"It should be stable, Admiral. Did the Mechs infiltrate our systems?"

"Negative," said Vernon. "Command and network integrity were maintained."

"Then I don't know, sir," said Davies. "I'd need to get back out there and take a look."

It was ten minutes since Davies had disabled the Mechs from the Firewall Sphere, yet already their limp metal bodies were being dragged away. Wounded bridge personnel were relieved and key positions filled. Stansfield surveyed the scene as he considered their next move.

"Charlie Team, what's your assessment of our current situation? Speak freely."

Ten responded first. He wasn't yet used to Stansfield's subtle combination of collaborative and commanding, but he rather liked it. Feeding into strategy had stimulated parts of his cloned brain that were long overdue a workout.

"I recommend we disable the Firewall Sphere, Admiral. It has firepower, serious firepower. We should get over there and strip them of supplies and secrets."

"I agree," said Hunter, who'd been stuffed full of food and drugs and seemed to be recovering. "We've gotta make sure we don't get some kind of resurrection from these things. If they suddenly wake up, we're right back where we started."

"There's hundreds of Mechs in that Sphere," pointed out Gray. "Dormant now, but way too many to shoot through the head. We would need another way of making sure they're disabled."

"I agree with Ten," said Davies. "We need to get some shuttles over there and start stripping the tech. There are some big guns on these things, can we dispatch tactical to see if we can use them? I want to know what that pulse was."

"Thank you, Charlie Team," said Stansfield. "That'll do for now. Get back to the Sphere and get to work. Conway, I want you to run the shuttle teams. Strip out weaponry in the Sphere and anything else you think might be useful. Charlie Team, have a good look around; anything you can see that we can use, let's have it. Vernon, I want a report on the cloning bay – get a team over there and let's make sure we're growing some new soldiers. If we have an issue with the signal to Sol, it might impact on the clones."

Vernon got right on it. Stansfield took a moment to consider the next move. It was years since he'd been in the heat of battle, but his time in stasis hadn't dulled his senses. Sol was wary of him, but what choice did they have? *Resolution, Conqueror* and *Orion* were on their way, and with them a whole new command structure that would displace his power soon enough. The Admiralty would want rid of his old Astute19 Class vessel at the earliest opportunity.

"Lieutenant Yau, in the absence of Davies I want to dispatch a small team to the shuttle to check on that comms signal. We must have somebody on board who can take a look?"

"Yes, sir. Maybe someone from Engineering?"

"Lieutenant Fernandez, report on our captured Mech friend, please," said Stansfield, opening a channel to the workshop.

There was no answer, and Stansfield frowned. "Fernandez, what's going on down there?"

No response, and the tension on the bridge was starting to grow.

"Get me a video feed," snapped Stansfield, drumming his fingers on the arm of his chair. "I want to see what's going on in that workshop."

Midshipman Khan worked quickly at the comms console, and moments later a hi-res feed from a camera in the corner of Fernandez's workshop flipped onto the main screen.

The images showed Lieutenant Fernandez backing away from a workshop table. A Mech lay on the table, its abdomen open and its innards exposed. The thing was still, dead and in pieces on its back.

But the top of its head was moving, separating from the body on eight spindly legs. The spider-thing heaved itself out of the Mech and stood for a moment on the table, turning one way then the other as Fernandez backed away.

Then it seemed to fix its attention on Fernandez, and it leapt across the room. Someone on the bridge screamed; others gasped in horror.

But the spider ran across the room, heading straight for

Fernandez as the lieutenant scuttled backwards as quickly as he could.

Then he had his pistol in his hand and was blasting away at the spider. One round tore away a leg, but the thing hardly slowed. Another struck its armoured carapace, and the spider cart-wheeled across the room to land on its back. For a moment it lay there, legs kicking; then it flipped itself over and spun back to face Fernandez.

But the delay had given the lieutenant time to aim properly, and his next shot went right through the spider, blowing a hole in its body. It shuddered and took a step back, but Fernandez came forward, aiming and firing as he moved, each round doing new damage.

And then it was done. Fernandez stood over the spider, breathing heavily, and tapped the shattered corpse with his foot.

"Dead," he said, voice shaking. "I think."

"What the hell was that, Fernandez?" snapped Stansfield, shaken by what he'd seen.

"The Mechs," said Fernandez, "they're some sort of hybrid creature with a semi-autonomous hunter-killer unit in the skull."

"Hunter-killer?" said Stansfield, his frown deepening. "Are you sure?"

"Not entirely, sir," said Fernandez, mechanically reloading his pistol while he spoke. "Are you seeing this with your Mechs?"

"*My* Mechs?" said Stansfield, not entirely understanding. Then his head whipped round to look at the corpses that still littered the edge of the bridge. Two teams were carrying them away, but it was slow work.

"There may be more of them with this ability," said Fernandez.

There was a soft *plunk* noise from a Mech on the far side of the bridge, and everyone turned to stare. Then the top of the Mech's head began to move as the spider-thing pulled itself free.

Stansfield shivered and drew his pistol, eyes fixed on the Mech. Then there was a second plunk, then a third, then a whole flurry from the corpses across the bridge.

"Oh, shit," said Stansfield.

2

Within moments, a dozen or more of the spider things had emerged from their hosts and were skittering across the deck on thin robotic legs. Each spider-like device had flat, pancake-shaped bodies and two red lights shone where eyes might be.

"Kill them," snapped Commander Vernon, firing his pistol at a spider that was running across the deck. Across the bridge, anybody with a weapon opened fire on the creatures. Vernon's target fountained brains and slewed to a halt, its legs twitching.

"Gotcha," snarled Vernon, but the other spider-Mechs were scuttling at speed towards vents, gaps and inlets.

The bridge crew fired where it was safe to do so, taking out several of the Mechs before they disappeared, but missing many others. In seconds, the bridge was clear and silent.

"Report," said Stansfield. "Any change in the Sphere, Davies?"

"Nothing I can see, sir."

"Fernandez, what's your status?"

"Two dead, Admiral. One injured, with a Mech attached to his face."

"Repeat that," said Vernon.

"It separated from the main body, then sprang off the floor and grabbed the back of Jeffreys' head. The legs are clamped around his skull, and oh, fuck!"

"Focus, Fernandez," said Stansfield, impatient and more than a little worried. "Details," he barked.

"Needles have come out the legs, and they've passed into Jeffreys' skull and the top of his spine. Oh, no." There was the sound of retching across the channel.

"Is Jeffreys conscious?" Vernon asked.

"Negative," said Fernandez, sounding distinctly unwell. "He's on the floor with this thing clamped round him. All it's doing is pulsing; I can see the Mech's own brain moving in its container. Should we tear the thing off?"

"No, don't do that, sir," said Davies urgently. "These are bio-mechanical entities, they'll need to be surgically removed. Have any other Bots done this?"

"No reports yet," said Yau, who was collating the sit-reps he was constantly receiving from all over the ship. "It seems any Mech that didn't have its head blown off has spawned one of these OctoBot things, and they've all scuttled off into vents and pipework. There are no further reports of cases like Jeffreys."

"Take Jeffreys to the medbay and place him in a secure containment area. He's to have a full guard on him. I want to know what that creature's doing to him. Charlie Team, what's your status?"

"Preparing to launch, sir," said Corporal Conway. "We're in the bay suiting up. Out in ten."

"Go faster," said Stansfield. "Keep me informed."

"Ay, sir," said Conway. "Out."

"Admiral, we have another problem," said Yau, his face telling a story. "We're getting reports of new power failures in some areas. Systems teams were getting the lighting back on, but that's been disabled, and we're back to emergency lighting."

"What are you trying to tell me?" growled Stansfield.

"It looks like the Bots are targeting our life support systems, sir. They've gone for power, air, water and temperature regulation. They're trying to close us down."

"And how long before that becomes a serious issue, lieutenant?" said Stansfield.

"Grant was the only one who really knew, sir," said Fernandez. In the background, they could hear the team moving Jeffreys. "He knew the ship like the back of his hand."

"Grant's not coming back," snapped Stansfield, "so give me what you have."

There was a pause before Fernandez spoke again. "Admiralty ship standards don't change much, but the Astute19 Class is a bit different from modern craft. Everything should have redundant backups, but power is key. If the fusion reactors are cut off or fail completely, we'll lose key systems as emergency power reserves are drained.

"Everything's modularised, so core power and the data integrity of the bridge are the last to go. Air is supplied as a priority to all personnel areas. Again, the bridge is last to go. Med areas are protected, as are key engineering and crew zones. Water's more of an inconvenience. At worst, we'd go to the recycling tanks and draw it directly. Power is a nuisance, but all essential systems are on back-up, and we can run core operations. Climate regulation is the first big issue; it's going to get stuffy very quickly."

"How long can we survive, Fernandez? Give me your best estimate?"

There was a pause before Fernandez answered. "If we don't use the engines, switch off the artificial gravity, and reduce use of non-essential systems, we might, with our current crew levels, survive for three weeks. It would be hot and airless, and we'd have to restrict areas bit by bit, to conserve oxygen."

"How long until we're joined by *Resolution*, *Conqueror* and *Orion*, Lieutenant?" said Stansfield, turning to Yau.

"If the portal reopens on schedule, sir, *Orion* could be here in as little as twenty-four hours, with *Resolution* and *Conqueror* arriving shortly after that later."

"Well, at least the Admiralty are taking this thing seriously," said Vernon.

"And what if they can't get through the portal?" said Stansfield.

"What if it fails to reopen, or they're destroyed as they emerge? We don't want a repeat of *Colossus*."

"Direct flight time," said Midshipman Kotter at the navigation console, "would be, ah." There was an awkward pause. "Seventy-four years from the nearest inhabited system. Longer, if they stopped to resupply."

There was a nasty silence on the bridge.

"We'd have to go back into stasis," said Vernon. It wasn't an option that anybody was keen to explore.

"With the systems in their current state," said Yau, "I don't think that would be possible. We don't have enough power."

"And we can't do anything while those things are running around the ship," said Stansfield. "We're going to have to send teams into the vents and conduits. We'll have to flush those things out and kill them."

Vernon made a face. That wasn't a job he'd wish on anyone.

Stansfield opened a channel. "New plan, Charlie Team. Hunter, Mason and Kearney report to the bridge. Marine X, Davies and Gray: get back to the Sphere. Start shutting it down and stripping it out. Conway, you have your orders already. Fernandez, let's get Jeffreys to the medbay ASAP."

"Roger," said Conway, "order received."

Then Yau spoke out on the bridge. "Something just changed in the Sphere, Admiral. Looks like power has returned to some systems."

"Move, Charlie Team," snapped Stansfield. "We're out of time."

"Roger," said Conway again. "Sixty seconds to departure. We'll take the fight to the enemy."

3
_____

"Rifle, pistols, ammunition, blade, backpack, power cells, grenades," muttered Ten as he walked through *Vengeance's* depleted armoury, picking out kit and loading it onto a trolley. He was back in his battered power armour, but he'd picked up a new HUD and the diagnostics had confirmed that the suit was in good working order, even though it was so ancient as to be obsolete.

"Like everything else on this ship," Ten said to himself as he checked over the rifle.

"You got enough stuff?" asked Davies, nodding at Ten's haul as he loaded his own suit with magazines and tech gear.

"For an operation of unknown duration behind enemy lines with vague operating parameters and a sketchy escape route?" said Ten as he taped magazines together. "No."

"When you put it like that," said Davies. Then he shrugged and went back to checking his own kit. "At least there's plenty of ammo," Davies went on.

Ten grunted and stuffed another pair of magazines into a side pocket of his backpack. They all had stories about running out of ammunition. It was one of the trials that they all shared, no matter what their rank or service.

"Better to have it and not need it," said Ten as he hefted the backpack. Heavy, but easily carried by the armour.

"Are you two old men ever going to be ready?" said Gray. "I'd like to get this done before my clone's use-by date." She was fully kitted and ready to go, a combat shotgun strapped to her pack alongside a heavy-duty tactical axe.

"It'll probably go mouldy and fail before we get back," said Jackson with a sad shake of his head. "Or you'll throw a joint under the weight of all that kit."

"Better than running short," snapped Gray, shaking her head at Jackson's selection.

"If you've quite finished," said Conway, hanging out the door of a shuttle, "then maybe we could get to work?"

Ten grinned as he tipped the rest of his kit into a second backpack, then threw both bags into the shuttle's passenger compartment. He stood aside as Gray, Jackson and Davies climbed aboard; then he smacked the control to close the doors.

"All aboard," he said jauntily. "Hey, Conway. There's a hole in the side of the Sphere, right? So we can get in?"

"Yes," said Conway in an exasperated tone as she ran through her pre-flight checks. "You saw it when we left. Why?"

Ten paused and looked around at the rest of the party, waiting till he had their full attention. Then he grinned.

"Once more unto the breach, dear friends," he said, settling back in his seat and closing his eyes, "once more."

The docking bay was empty when Conway guided the shuttle in through the door. The team watched in silence as she manoeuvred the tiny craft through the vast volume before setting it gently down near an airlock.

The team cycled quickly out of the shuttle's airlock and made their way across the bay and into the Sphere's interior. Ten took the lead, following his rifle through the inner airlock door into the dark and gloomy space beyond.

"The moment you see any movement, shout," said Ten as he pushed away a Mech corpse that had floated along the corridor. He wasn't happy to be back aboard the Sphere, but at least this time they weren't improvising their weapons.

With Conway in the shuttle, Marine X, Gray, Jackson and Davies were exploring the Sphere, moving carefully into the corridors. They cycled through an airlock and all of a sudden there was noise.

"Gray, Jackson, go that way," said Ten, pointing down a corridor. "Davies and I will go this way, and we'll meet up further down."

"Roger," said Gray, moving into the corridor, her armoured bulk following her rifle.

"Probably never be able to find you," said Jackson as he followed Gray. Ten watched them float away, then spun to follow Davies.

"I've got movement up ahead," said Davies. "Mechs, more than one. Dammit, why did it have to be me? I'm supposed to be the tech guy."

"They're cyborgs, Double-D," said Ten with a smirk. "They're bound to go for you."

"What's happening, Davies?" came Stansfield's voice over the comms channel.

"There's a lot of dead Mechs floating around, sir. No idea how many are left, but we can hear them moving around and separating, just like you described. Hell, I can hear their creepy little legs tapping on metal."

"Do what you must, Davies, but get me the tech. We're going through the files Hunter retrieved, but we need the hardware as well if we're to get answers."

"Roger," said Davies unhappily. He switched channels. "Did you do all this?" he said to Ten, gesturing at the bullet holes in the walls and the corpses in the air.

"Some," admitted Ten. "Seemed like a good idea at the time," he said, brushing away a loop of intestine. Then they came to an open door.

"Tech area," said Davies, pulling himself in to take a look around.

It was a mess. The consoles and machinery were in good condition, but a Mech corpse had floated in through the door, pulled by the air currents, and had lodged against a fabricator.

"Can you get anything out of that?" asked Ten, nodding at a console.

Davies made his way through the tech area to hang in front of an undamaged console.

"Probably," he said, taking a dongle from his waist pouch and searching for a port into which to fit it. "Dammit," he said, struggling to reach the port. Space was tight, and the power armour kept getting in the way. He slipped off his helmet and set it on the console, then pulled himself under the desk.

"Thank fuck for open standards and lax security protocols," he muttered as he found a matching port and plugged in the dongle. "These protocols are all ancient Earth tech," said Davies. "I've got a nice little kit of tools that'll chop through their firewalls faster than a hot curry through a Labrador."

"You've got a what?" said Ten.

"Files," said Davies. "Old ones, ancient ones and cutting-edge stuff that nobody's supposed to have outside the labs. All sorts of counter-espionage stuff dating back about three-hundred years."

"Right," said Ten with a frown, "and that's useful because...?"

"Probably isn't," Davies admitted as he worked, "but it's sort of a hobby, you know? Like collecting old pistols or medieval swords."

Systems information began to appear in his HUD, and he whistled as he searched for items of interest, flicking down the list and delving into the sub-branches.

"Don't need it here, of course, 'cos they're using old, insecure tech. It's just a question of choosing," he said. Then he nodded. "Reckon we'll just have the lot," he said as Ten floated back into the corridor. A couple of tweaks, and the dongle started copying every file it could find. "Ninety seconds," said Davies, looking around the room. The air was musty, smelling of a nasty mixture of oil and sewage, and Davies wrinkled his nose.

Then he looked again at the Mech that floated above the console, held in place by its own trailing guts. It spun gently, until Davies could see its head and the spot where an OctoBot had detached from the skull. Not good.

And suddenly all he could hear was the light, metallic echo of magnetic OctoBot legs on metal as they scurried around, unseen in the darkened room.

"We're not alone in here," whispered Davies.

Then, to his side, there was movement on top of one of the units.

An OctoBot came scrabbling along a surface. Davies scrambled for his rifle, but before he could bring it to bear, the OctoBot had leapt. Clearly these things had no trouble operating in zero-G.

Davies turned, flailing in mid-air, and the thing missed his face. But it found his arm, and immediately took a firm grip.

"Help," squeaked Davies, tearing at the thing with his free hand, banging it hard against the side of a metal casing in an attempt to dislodge it.

The OctoBot moved one of its legs, and a needle shot out of the end. It reminded Davies of the scorpions he'd seen at one of his cadet briefings. Their academy tutor had warned them to keep away from the creatures. The OctoBot had eight stings, and Davies didn't fancy his chances.

He smashed the creature on a wall and spun away as the needle retracted. He needed a knife or something to stab it with, but he'd loaded up with tech, ammunition and power rather than old-fashioned blades.

For a moment, the OctoBot released all but two of its legs, easing the pressure on Davies' arm. He flung it away, then bounced gently off the ceiling, steadying himself on a fitting with his free arm.

The OctoBot banged off a console and disappeared. Davies tried to push himself in the other direction, aiming for the door out into the corridor.

But he couldn't get a good purchase on the ceiling, and then the OctoBot hit him in the chest, spinning him around. Davies yelped again as the creature scurried over his armour onto his face. He put one hand over his mouth in an attempt to stop the thing from smothering him. His other hand scrabbled at it as he tried to rip it away.

"Davies, hold still, let me take the shot."

It was Conway. She must have followed them in. She was braced against the doorway, rifle aimed and a finger hovering over the trigger.

"You'll take my freaking head off," he screamed as she steadied the weapon, waiting for a clear shot.

"Trust me," she said quietly, trying to calm him. "I've got your back."

"Like you had Gallagher's?"

The OctoBot had two needles ready to plunge deep into Davies' skull, and its other six legs were edging around his skull, tightening their grip.

"Hold still, dammit. To the side!"

"Fuck," he shouted in a muffled voice as the OctoBot squeezed. He could barely see, but he snatched at a mounting point on the ceiling and slewed to a halt, turning his head to give Conway a decently clear shot.

There was a shot, then another, and the main weight of the OctoBot fell away, blasted free, leaving the legs clamped around Davies' head.

He clawed mindlessly at the legs, with no idea of which way was which or where Conway was. There was more gunfire, then sudden quiet. He opened his eyes and saw Conway still braced against the doorway, a cloud of gun smoke dispersing in front of her.

Davies looked at her with a weak grin and started breathing once again.

"If you ever mention Gallagher to me again like that, I'll take your head off, Bot or no Bot. You hear me, Davies?"

"Sorry. I'm a dickhead, I didn't mean it. It was either say that or shit my pants. I should have just shit my pants."

"Collect your weapon, put your helmet back on, and get back to work."

Conway was pissed, really pissed. It had been a long time since Davies had seen her that way. He'd been out of order, and he knew it.

Then there was a sudden electrical hum and the lamps came back on, bathing the room in light.

"Argh!" said Davies as the gravity came on as well and he crashed to the floor. He rolled onto his back just in time to see Ten saunter through the doorway.

"Gravity's back," he announced as Davis groaned. "Did I miss something?"

Conway just shook her head.

"We got a visit from our eight-legged friends," said Davies. "Anyone else, or was it just me?"

"We've seen a couple," Gray replied. "But they're going a bit crazy."

"Me too," said Ten. "They're like bats in a cave. I had a couple try to jump me, but the rest of them don't seem to know I'm here. They're all crawling up the inside of this thing and making their way to the ceiling area. They're clustering there, completely still, just stuck on the ceiling."

"Seen that as well," said Gray. "I had to kill a few that were on the walkways, but the others are just scuttling off."

"Probably waiting to ambush us," said Jackson, "like drop-bears in Australia."

"Pretty sure that's an urban myth," said Conway, frowning.

"Download's complete," said Davies quietly as he retrieved the dongle and refitted his helmet. "That'll give us everything Hunter didn't manage to snatch."

"What's your plan, Ten?" Gray asked.

"Backtrack to our position. We'll stick together from here."

"We'll cover less ground," said Jackson. "Might not be able to find everything we need."

"Maybe," agreed Ten, "but less chance of being ambushed." He looked at Conway, who was glaring at him from within her helmet. "That okay with you, Corporal?"

She snorted. "They're as far outside my command chain as yours, Ten. Let's just get the job done."

Ten nodded. "Roger." He flicked open another channel. "You getting everything, *Vengeance*?"

"Much clearer with the lights on," said Yau. "Following your every move and tapping away at my console."

Ten led the team out of the tech room as soon as Gray and Jackson arrived. They could hear the Mechs moving in the corridors, but they saw nothing.

"It's as if they're keeping away from us," said Gray after they'd gone a hundred metres.

"Gathering at a pinch point to launch a devastating attack," was Jackson's unsurprising assessment.

"We're almost at the edge of the sphere," said Ten a few moments later. "It's the first time I've got a close look at this thing. It looks like it's made out of scrap. Seriously, it looks like they welded a load of old spaceships together to build this."

"Keep it coming, Marine X, we love a good story," said Fernandez.

"Heading out into the open," reported Ten as the team left the central structure and moved out onto a gantry that connected to the inner surface of the sphere, fifty metres away. It was darker out here, away from the overhead lights, but the AI-enhanced night-vision in their HUDs picked out the details.

"This thing is vast. I can see the OctoBots; they're all following the same path to the top of the Sphere. They're like ants making their way back to a nest."

"What the hell are they doing up there?" asked Gray, sighting along her rifle at the distant bots.

"Is that writing?" asked Conway. She was looking at something on the wall above them, twisting her head to try to make it out.

"Yes," said Ten, his voice cold. "It's writing, definitely writing."

And then Stansfield was in the channel. "Is it human, Marine X? Can you tell?"

"I said this thing looked like it was made from old battleships. I'm sending you a visual via my HUD now. Do you see that, *Vengeance*?"

"It's too dark," said Yau. "I can't make it out."

"It's an old Sol ship," said Ten, his tone flat with horror. "Those words come from its hull. A ship's name, stamped into the steel."

"What ship?" barked Stansfield. "Marine X! What's the ship's name?"

"It's *Centurion*, sir," whispered Ten. "We've found *Centurion*."

4

Ten made certain that *Vengeance* had received a decent image of the large, painted name plate from *Centurion*; then he continued his survey of the Sphere's inner wall.

"Should have brought some drones," muttered Ten as he played his HUD cameras across the inside of the Sphere, working steadily towards the top. "Looks like there are a hundred, maybe a hundred and thirty, OctoBots up there. They're just clustering, though, I don't understand it."

"Are you okay, Ten?" asked Gray, edging closer.

"Take a look up there," said Ten, nodding at the top of the Sphere. "Zoom your HUD, night-vision your view. Do you see it?"

"Do I see–" said Gray. "Whoa, yes, I see it. That's weird."

"Are you getting this, *Vengeance*? Right at the top of the Sphere, there's a huge circular dish. Just looks like the top of the Sphere is in shadow when you're looking from down below, but it's like a comms dish. It keeps tilting slightly, like it's fixing on a signal. And the Octo-Bots are all connecting with it, it's surrounded by plug-in slots."

"Mr Davies, any theories?" Stansfield asked.

"Yeah, sounds to me like they're getting updates from the mother ship."

"I've gotta tell you, sir," Gray chipped in, "it certainly looks that way. There's some sort of mechanical operation going on as well. They're plugging themselves in around the dish, and something is changing their bodies, adding components. Then they just scuttle off and wait."

"I think Davies might be right," said Ten. "Take a closer look at Bots that have disconnected."

"Are those ... wings?" whispered Gray, unable to keep a trace of fear from her voice.

"You've got to be shitting me," said Jackson as he stared up at the distant roof of the Sphere. "The fuckers fly now?"

"I think they've seen us," said Ten as upgraded OctoBots dropped off the ceiling and snapped open their wings. They flapped around like large, inelegant bats searching for prey, swooping ever lower. "Are you any good with a fly swat, Gray?"

"No," said Gray. "I'm not. Will a shotgun do?"

"I certainly hope so. Get under cover," Ten said, backing along the walkway and firing at the swooping bots.

Gray and Jackson opened fire, but as the bots began to dive, it became difficult to select a target. One by one, slowly at first but ever more quickly, the bots completed their upgrades and dropped from the ceiling, like bats leaving a cave in search of food.

They formed squadrons as they fell, flying in clusters of ten to swoop quickly towards the Marines as they edged along the walkway.

"A flamethrower would be really fucking useful right now," said Ten as the team shuffled back, firing as they went. "Or a shotgun."

"At least they're not shitting on us," said Jackson. "Couldn't cope with that."

"Does that look like a bombing run?" asked Conway as she fired at a cluster of Bots that were diving towards the team.

Ten stared for a moment, mouth open. "Run," he yelled, ignoring his own advice to fire at the rapidly advancing bots. The rest of the team turned and ran as Ten emptied his magazine into the approaching cluster. Then he was after them, sprinting along the walkway toward the doors that led back into the super-structure.

Davies pushed open the doors and turned to fire over Ten's head, one foot wedged against the floor to hold the way open for the other Marines. Gray, Jackson and Conway dived past him as Ten sprinted along.

But the bots were fast, much faster than a Marine in power armour, and they flashed over Ten's head, releasing dozens of little bomblets as they went, then soared up to avoid crashing into the buildings.

For a moment it looked like nothing would happen. The bomblets bounced across the steel plates of the walkway or pinged harmlessly off Ten's armour.

Then they exploded, all at once, swallowing Ten in a cloud of flame and smoke. There was a terrible crash as the plating of the walkway was torn away, and the team were peppered with shrapnel and debris.

"Ten!" yelled Davies, appalled at the sight. He thrashed his arm uselessly at the smoke, switching his HUD to infrared so that he could peer through the murk.

"Ten?" said Conway, checking Ten's medical information in her HUD. "He's not showing up dead," she said, faintly surprised.

"There, look," said Davies, pointing into the smoke. The team stared at an armoured glove that clutched at the blackened metal of the walkway.

"Help," squeaked Ten. "Need some help."

Conway and Jackson surged forward, charging into the smoke. Ten was hanging from a twisted beam, swinging gently.

"Give me your hand," said Conway, throwing herself down onto the walkway so that she could reach down for Ten's free hand.

Jackson slung his weapon and crouched down, clamping his hand around Ten's wrist as Conway took his other hand.

"Had something lined up for just this situation," wheezed Ten as he was hauled back to safety.

"Heard it," snapped Conway as she helped Ten to his feet. "And this is no time for jokes."

"Thanks," said Ten, looking around for his rifle. "Must have bloody dropped it in the excitement," he murmured, pulling out a pistol.

"Time's up," yelled Davies suddenly. "You need to move, now!"

Ten looked around and saw that more clusters of OctoBots had formed. The first had already begun another bombing run.

This time, nobody stopped to return fire or contemplate the ineffable; they just ran into the Sphere's super-structure and slammed the doors behind them. They clattered down the corridor as bomblets bounced off the doors. Moments later, there was another explosion, and the doors were pummelled into the corridor. The air filled with shrapnel, and the team slid as one around a corner.

"Tough stuff, this armour," said Ten as they paused to take stock.

"It's not going to be enough to get us out of here," said Jackson as he reloaded his rifle.

"We can't go that way," said Gray, nodding at the corner, "so where now?"

"Didn't you find an armoury when you were first here?" said Conway. "Maybe they have flamethrowers, or something else we can use against these flying fuckers."

Ten shrugged. "Not the worst idea I've ever heard, but a bit optimistic. Anything useful on *Vengeance*?"

Davies snorted. "We already have everything they had on *Vengeance*. Bloody ship's an antiquated junkshop. No, we're on our own."

"Armoury it is, then," said Ten, "but I'm not hopeful. And it's that way," he said, pointing back down the corridor.

"Past the flying OctoBots of doom," said Jackson with a sigh, "because there's no better way to round off a shitty day."

"Quit whining," snapped Conway, checking her weapon. "We've had sixty seconds of downtime, now get back to work. You and me to the junction, clear the corridor, then across with the others."

"Corp," acknowledged Jackson. "Let's do this!"

Jackson and Conway moved to the edge of the junction and then flowed around the corner, rifles up and spitting fire into the smoke-filled corridor before the OctoBots knew what was happening. Ten,

Gray and Davies crossed the corridor and scanned the way ahead; then Conway and Jackson rolled into cover and everything was suddenly quiet.

"Got a couple," said Conway as she reloaded her rifle, "but they're clustering again. It'll be no more than minutes before they attack."

"And we're still getting movement pings," said Davies, "so I reckon there are other Mechs active up ahead."

"Better get going, then," said Ten, leading the way along the corridor. Davies and Jackson followed, with Gray and Conway making up the rear-guard.

"The armoury should be down this way, then left," said Ten as they moved through the corridor.

"This is too easy," said Jackson. "Where are they all?"

"Movement," said Davies, "movement up ahead, coming this way."

Then they all heard it: the distinctive sound of OctoBots running across the floors or along the walls.

"Steady," said Ten, taking another step forward, pistol raised. "Stay sharp."

Then there was a flurry of scuttling noises and the corridor was suddenly full of OctoBots, all scurrying along.

"Contact," yelped Ten as he fired at the targets his HUD was struggling to count. Lots of noise from behind as the rest of the team opened fire; then Ten had time only to yell in shock as an OctoBot came for him at head height, legs outstretched and reaching for him.

5

The OctoBot smacked into the visor of Ten's helmet and grabbed at his head. Two of the thing's legs were armed with diamond-tipped drills, and the bits skittered and screeched across Ten's armour as the OctoBot searched for a way in.

He staggered back, thick armoured fingers groping at the OctoBot and sliding across its shell as he struggled to get a grip. He shook his head as the drill bits danced across the toughened surface of the armour, but it was only a matter of time before they caught a rim or cut into the metal.

"Get it off," yelled Ten, battering at his head with his fists, trying to crush the OctoBot before it could do any damage.

"Stop jumping around, you daft bugger," said Conway, rifle ready but unable to shoot.

Ten's fingers ripped at the OctoBot, pulling away a pair of legs, but not moving the creature's body at all.

"Argh!" he said, pounding at the OctoBot's hull and trying to crush it. He stumbled across the floor and bounced off a wall.

Then he had an idea. He turned quickly, charged across the corridor, and rammed his helmet into the wall, relying on the armour's structural integrity to protect his neck and head from harm. There was a crack, and the OctoBot's drills paused their hunt.

Ten smashed himself against the wall once more, and the Octo-Bot's hull failed completely. He grabbed at the thing, this time gaining a solid grip, and ripped it from his helmet. It left behind a thick smear of blood and brain material, which dribbled down across his visor before freezing solid in the frigid air. He tossed it away and it clattered across the floor.

"Ten," said Conway, grabbing him by the shoulders. "Are you okay?"

"Fine," said Ten, shaking his head. He staggered back a step and tumbled to the floor. "Long day," he muttered, wiping a gloved hand across his visor in a vain attempt to clear it.

There was a sudden bang of gunfire as Gray finished off the Octo-Bot. She kicked the corpse along the corridor, then turned back to Ten. "Leave me to do all the work, why don't you?" she said.

Ten took a moment before he got up off the floor. "You know how it is, a Marine has to catch his forty winks wherever he can."

From behind Gray floated the sound of rapid gunfire as Jackson and Davies took apart the flying OctoBots that were still battering their way into the corridor.

"We've killed shitloads of them," said Conway, "but they're still coming."

"Movement further down the way," warned Gray.

"Where'd the others go?" said Ten as he joined Gray to inspect the corridor ahead. "There were dozens of the buggers a moment ago."

"Not a good sign," said Jackson, backing along the corridor and reloading his rifle. "They'll be back soon enough."

Ten nodded . "What now?"

"Check in," said Conway with a shrug. "Update Stansfield, find out what he wants us to do next." She opened a channel to *Vengeance*.

"The OctoBots have drills as well as needles," said Conway, "so watch out even if you're wearing armour. What do you want us to do, Admiral? Stay here or head back to *Vengeance*?"

"Stay there," said Stansfield, "and take a good look around. Focus on weaponry and defensive systems, then power sources and tech. We need to understand as much as we can about the spheres and their builders."

"Acknowledged, sir. If you need any help flushing out those Bots from *Vengeance*, you know where we are. Don't let them get anywhere near your head, they don't let you go once they're clamped on."

"Appreciate the advice," said Mason. "We're about to start flushing the vents."

"Be careful in there," Gray cautioned. "They're fast and furious."

"These things are ambush specialists, they'll be looking to shock," said Ten. "So wear the brown trousers."

"**D**uly noted," Kearney said as she completed preparations to begin clearing Bots from the battleship. "Are we cleared to enter, Bridge?"

"You're cleared," confirmed Vernon. "We've got four clusters of Bots on the ship. Three are straightforward. They're in the tech zone, around the cloning bays and in the central vents near the support systems. The cluster around the ship's core is trickier. The OctoBots appear to be waiting. Whatever they were doing earlier, they've stopped, and there's been no sign of movement or system disruption. Yet."

"I'm assigning one team to each of the three easier clusters," said Stansfield. "We'll need to approach the core with more caution because of the sensitive nature of the equipment; we could take out the entire ship if we mess that up. We'll leave it for last. Charlie Team, you'll each take one team. Hunter to tech, Kearney to support systems. Mason, you need to clear the cloning bays. We've lost the connection to the pods, so we've no idea what's going on down there."

"Roger," said Mason grimly. The thought that the OctoBots might have unrestricted access to the cloning pods was most unwelcome.

"We've assigned five Marines to each team."

"You're assigning me a team?" Hunter asked, surprised.

"Indeed I am, Trooper," said Stansfield, not sounding happy about it. "And I expect you to do a damned good job, but remember that I have the remote for the thing in your head. The Bots are the least of your problems if you do anything to remind me of why you're a Penal Marine. We're clear on that, yes?"

"Sir," said Hunter.

"Alright, Troopers, off you go," ordered Vernon. "Keep the command channels open, and don't skimp on the updates. Your teams are assembling one level down."

As soon as Charlie Team had cleared the bridge, Stansfield dismissed them from his mind and returned his attention to the ship. *Vengeance* was in a bad way. "Lieutenant Yau, what's the status on our repairs? Can we get an analysis of the images from the Sphere? And are we any closer to identifying those pulses?"

Stansfield was straight back to business, and the bridge was beginning to return to normality, but the damage to the doors was a constant reminder of how close they'd come to being overrun by the Mechs.

"Almost there, sir. I've sent Conway's data to Sol, but the interference on the line is bad, and I've had nothing back yet. *Orion* will be with us in a matter of hours."

"Thank you, Lieutenant," said Vernon, walking over to Stansfield. "I'm going down to personally supervise the ejection of the Mechs into space. I want to make sure we get every last one of them."

"Yes, do that, Ed. Check on the cloning bay, too. It's been left unattended since Davies re-activated the link. If we've got a new enemy on the way, we'll need more bodies, and I'll take them from *Orion*, from the other ships or from the cloning bays. We're in no fit state to fight any battles at the moment."

"Will do, sir."

Vernon left the bridge, heading for the cloning bays, and Stansfield settled back in his chair. He pulled up the feed from Charlie Team, and watched as they set about clearing his ship of Bots.

"We'll split into groups of three," said Kearney as she briefed her team of Marines. "The Bots are clustered here," she went on, dropping a pin in her HUD as she briefed her team. "We go in here" – she dropped another pin – "and we're going to drive the Bots out of the vents into an airlock, then blast them into space. We'll use vent maintenance drones as bait," she said, pointing at the stack of crated drones waiting to be deployed.

She saw the Marines share a sceptical glance. "You don't think this will work?"

Brewis shrugged, obviously sceptical. "Maybe, but I don't fancy chasing them through the vents. That's nasty work."

"Nasty," agreed Kearney, "but necessary. And Arthur here is going to tell us how to make it work."

Midshipman Arthur blinked in surprise and frowned at Kearney. "It won't work," she said simply. "The Bots are in processing plant number two, it's four hundred cubic metres in a T-shaped layout, and there's no way to vent directly from there into the airlock. Can't be done."

"But there are pipes from the plant to the airlock," said Kearney. "I've seen the plans."

"Yes, half-metre-diameter pipes," said Arthur slowly, as if explaining to a child, "but they empty into compressors and storage tanks, not the plant itself."

Kearney brought up the plans and shoved them onto the shared channel. "These," she said, dropping a pin on the plan, "are access doors from the plant to the pipes. That's how we do it. We open the access doors, then encourage the Bots into the pipes using low-power flamethrowers in the plant," she said. "Once they're in the pipes, we close the access doors, open the airlock and blast them into space. Simple."

"Why would they go into the pipes?" asked Sanders. "These things aren't stupid."

"Doesn't matter," said Arthur, shaking her head, "because there are emergency valves in the pipes. Open the airlock doors, and the valves close to stop air escaping."

"So we lock them open–" began Kearney.

"Doesn't work like that," interrupted Arthur. "Can't force the valves to stay open. They're independently powered and autonomous."

"So we wedge them open," said Kearney through gritted teeth, "and we're good to go."

Arthur raised an eyebrow. "It'd have to be done manually, from inside the pipes, and there's no room for armour."

"And we still need to get the damned things into the pipes," pointed out Sanders.

Kearney was silent for a moment; then she nodded. "Right. Two of us to fix the pipes, the rest in the plant, and Arthur controlling the airlock. Here's how we'll do it."

She sketched out her plan, then looked around at the Marines. They weren't impressed.

"Whose turn is it to engage in mortal jeopardy?" asked Sanders, looking at Brewis.

"Yeah," Brewis said despondently, "that'll be me."

"You have a rota?" said Kearney, morbidly fascinated.

"Sure," said Sanders, "saves someone acting the hero all the time."

"You guys are unbelievable," muttered Kearney with a shake of her head. "Ten minutes to suit up, then we go."

Fifteen minutes later, Kearney and Brewis were in the airlock looking at the air pipes. They were both wearing the lightest shirts and shorts they could find, with low-calibre pistols and compact flame-throwers strapped across their chests. They'd locked open the valves that emptied into the airlock, but neither was keen to climb into the pipes.

"We're ready down here," said Sanders.

Kearney acknowledged him and looked around at Arthur, who was standing outside the airlock. The inner door stood open: their escape route, once they'd done the job.

"Left," said Kearney as they stood before the pipes, "or right?"

"Does it matter?" said Brewis.

"I'll take the left," said Kearney, heaving herself into the pipe. Along with her weapons, she carried two stout bars with which to jam open the valves. "See you on the other side."

She pulled herself along the pipe, making as little noise as possible. It was dark, lit only by the tiny lamps on her HUD, and cramped. After five metres, it was also stuffy and hot. Arthur had insisted on turning off the fans.

The vent was just big enough to crawl along on knees and elbows, but it was hard work. It was also filthy with years of dust, debris and rat droppings.

"You're coming up on the first valve," said Arthur, who was monitoring their positions on a data slate. "You see it?"

"Yeah," said Brewis as he squeezed past. "Fitting the bar now."

"Done mine," said Kearney.

"Testing," said Arthur. "Yup, they're both jammed."

"On we go," muttered Kearney, forcing herself deeper into the pipe and trying not to think about having to fight her way out.

They passed the second valve without difficulty, then arrived at the emergency access plate. This was the nasty, dangerous part of the plan, and Kearney was no keener on it than Brewis had been during the briefing.

"No other option," muttered Kearney. "In position," she said. Seconds later, Brewis confirmed his readiness.

"We're going in," said Sanders. The rest of the Marines were suited in full power armour, all armed with flame-throwers and carrying rifles and spare ammo. "We've found the Bots. They're clustered near the access hatches to the pipes."

"Oh, good," said Brewis.

"Shit, they're moving," said Sanders. "Flame away, herd them back. Time for the bait."

"Roger," said Kearney. "Hit it, Arthur."

There was a crack as the age-old seals broke on the access hatches, then a squeal of tortured hydraulics as the curved panels, each a metre long and covering half the pipe, were levered up.

Kearney popped out into the blessedly cool air of the processing plant just as Brewis appeared in the hatch to the other pipe.

"We're here," she said, looking around, flame-thrower in her hand, "but I don't see–"

Then an OctoBot dropped onto the pipe three metres from where she sat and turned to stare at her. It was joined by a second, then a third.

"Shit," muttered Kearney, not daring to move.

Then there was a rush of noise and a burst of heat as flames sprayed a little too close for comfort.

"Shit," yelled Kearney as more OctoBots appeared. One dropped down into the pipe to get away from the heat, and suddenly Kearney remembered what she was supposed to do. "It's working," she said, before diving back into the pipe and crawling for the airlock.

She glanced back as she heard metallic footsteps in the pipe. They were following, but that no longer seemed like a good thing. She crawled faster, heaving herself through the first valve, then snatching another glance back.

"Fuck," she yelled, rolling onto her back and grabbing at the flame-thrower. She aimed it back down the pipe, which now boiled with OctoBots, and pushed against the pipe with her feet to squirm her way to safety. She half sat up, bracing her head against the top of the pipe, and squeezed the trigger. A jet of flame shot down the pipe and rolled over the OctoBots.

Something screamed, and for a moment Kearney thought it might have been dying OctoBots. Then she realised it was her, and that she'd scorched her inner thighs and calves. The OctoBots were still coming, clearly fearing the flames in the plant more than the flames in the pipe.

Kearney threw the flamethrower at them and began to push her way along the pipe as fast as she could go. An OctoBot grabbed at her boot and she kicked it away; then she smacked at another as it tried to race along the top of the pipe.

"Too close," she muttered, drawing her pistol. She paused, emptied the magazine into the mass of OctoBots, then turned and scrambled along the pipe, heedless of the enemies behind her and desperate only to escape. She could hear them at her heels, then she was at the mouth of the pipe and Arthur was in front of her with a rifle.

Kearney heaved herself out and flopped to the floor of the airlock as Arthur blazed away, firing the weapon on full auto until the magazine was empty.

"Go," screamed Arthur, reloading the weapon and sliding over to look along Brewis' pipe. "Brewis, move!"

"Can't get clear," said Brewis, and the sound of pistol fire echoed along the pipe. "Argh, they're all over me." He screamed again, a sound of pain and fear as the OctoBots swarmed over him and cut into his flesh.

"Come on," said Kearney, dragging Arthur across the airlock. "Nothing we can do but finish the plan."

Arthur nodded dumbly and stumbled across the airlock as a pair of OctoBots emerged from Kearney's pipe and skittered across the floor.

"Go," screamed Kearney, and they both tumbled through the door into the corridor. Arthur mashed the power button and the airlock doors slammed shut.

"Status," said Kearney as she peered in through the airlock windows. OctoBots were piling into the room from both pipes, scores of them.

"We're clear," said Sanders. "No living Bots left here."

"Close the access hatches," said Kearney to Arthur.

"Roger," said Arthur, hands shaking so badly she could hardly grip the data slate. She fumbled at it for a few seconds as Kearney watched anxiously; then she nodded. "Done. Airlock?"

"Do it," said Kearney with an exhausted nod.

Arthur punched another button and the outer doors slid open. Air streamed down the pipes, tugging at the teeming pile of OctoBots. For a moment, Kearney thought it wasn't going to work. Then one of the Bots lost its footing, and bounced and tumbled its way across its fellows and out of the airlock door. Another followed, then five more, and Brewis' remains went with them, blasted out of the airlock as Arthur restarted the fans and cranked up the airflow.

Seconds later, the airlock was empty, and Arthur closed the doors.

"Good work, people," said Kearney. "Are we clear there, Leman?"

"No sign of Bots in the processing plant or the pipes. We're clear," came the reply.

"Good job, Kearney," came Stansfield's voice over the radio. "Get your team down to the cloning bays."

"Ay, sir," said Kearney wearily, "on our way."

"Brewis' mind state is secure," reported Sanders. "He's in the queue for redeployment."

Kearney closed her eyes and leant back against the wall. She didn't envy Brewis his nightmares, but at least he'd be alive to have them.

"Guess we'd better get down to the bays, then," she said, eyes still closed, "so that we've got somewhere to redeploy him."

6

Mason and his team arrived at the newly installed cloning bays and stopped to survey the situation. The bays had been assembled in a hurriedly-cleared storage bay, and there were giant access doors at either end.

"That doesn't look good," said Mason as he peered through the inspection windows in one set of doors. The bays were completely standard, as found across Commonwealth space. Behind them were tanks of chemicals, connected by thick pipes to the pods where the clones would be grown and the personalities deployed.

"We're at the cloning bay," said Mason, "and we've got a problem. Are you seeing this?"

"Seeing," said Stansfield from the bridge, "but not understanding."

"The OctoBots have done something weird, sir. They've somehow joined together," said Mason, "and now there's just one huge Bot sitting over the clone conduits."

"Elucidate, please," said Stansfield.

"It's like they all dismantled and used the parts to build a bigger bot," said Mason. "There's about twenty of them, so this thing has twenty brains and who knows how many legs. Each leg appears to have connected to the data conduits for the cloning bay. This isn't looking good."

"Vernon, are you into the cloning bays yet?" Stansfield asked.

"We're at the second doors. Our teams here are just breaking through," said Vernon. "These ones were sealed during the fighting. Won't be long now, will report back soon."

"What's the story, Wilkins?" said Mason. Wilkins, a Marine tech specialist, had linked his data slate to the local cloning pod control network inside the engineering bay, and was running diagnostics to work out what was going on.

"The pods are active, but they're not running one of our standard programmes."

"So what are they running?" asked Mason, frowning at the pods.

"No idea," said Wilkins. "but it looks like they're almost finished. You want me to disrupt it?"

"Yeah, switch it off," said Mason. "Whatever it is, it ain't friendly."

"Roger, done," said Wilkins, tapping at his slate. "Hmm, that's not good." He poked some more, then shook his head. "Disconnected. Whatever that thing is, it knows we're here and it's locked us out."

Inside the bay, the MegaBot shifted on the pods.

"Back to Plan A, then," said Mason, hefting one of the sonic disruptors they'd retrieved from the armoury. They were normally used for siege-breaking or crowd control, emitting extremely loud noises to discomfort organic lifeforms. "Am I blowing it or leaving it in the ship, sir?" he asked. "I'm going to have to recalibrate the sonic disruptors if they stand any chance against this thing, but I think it might work."

"Terminate it, Mason," Stansfield ordered. "We can't permit anything to interfere with the cloning bays."

"On it now, Admiral."

"I'm going in alone," said Hunter, after he'd assessed the situation. "I'm going to use a handy tool in my arm attachment to deal with them."

"Negative, Hunter," said Stansfield. "This is not a one-person job."

"Permission to speak freely, Admiral?" Hunter asked.

"Go ahead," Stansfield replied.

"I've taken a look at the schematics down there. Those vents are lined with cables. We can't use flame-throwers or guns without trashing your infrastructure. I can deliver precision blows to the bots without causing further damage to the ship. I'd like to give it a try, sir."

Hunter hadn't expected a positive reception.

"Agreed. But the moment you get into trouble, we're sending in support after you."

"Thanks, Admiral. Going in now." He turned to the Marines of his team. "Cover me," he said, "and if this all goes wrong, well, you know the drill."

"No worries," said Sergeant Rodha, hefting his rifle as he and his Marines stood clear of the vents. None of them had been keen to work with Hunter, whose reputation for reckless disobedience was well known.

The Marines watched as Hunter stretched his neck and checked his cybernetic arm was fully charged. He was wearing combat fatigues, and his only concession to personal safety was a light anti-stab vest and a large piece of fine steel mesh that was little more than cosmetic.

"You sure about this?" asked Rodha, nodding at the vent and giving the mesh the hairy eyeball.

Hunter gave him a flat stare, then shrugged. "You got a better idea?"

Rodha sniffed and shook his head.

"Just keep an eye on things out here," said Hunter as he eased himself into the vent, "and let me know if anything nasty comes looking for me."

"Sure," said Rodha with a nod.

Hunter squeezed his way into the vent and used his HUD to both show him the way ahead and keep up a running commentary on the team's channel.

This vent was slightly more hospitable to human movement than others on the ship, but it was still cramped, dark and dirty with the grime of decades.

At the end of the vent, Hunter peered into one of the engineering bays. A whole bunch of OctoBots had clustered amongst a pile of discarded crates that were waiting for recycling.

"No MegaBots down here, I'm pleased to say," after a few minutes' crawling, "just a big nest of the little fuckers. I'm going to activate a tool on my arm, right, and if anybody wants their porridge cooking, now's the time to shout. Anybody? No? Here goes, then."

He blocked the vent with the mesh and poked his cybernetic fist through a gap, pointing it at the clustered bots. His arm made an electronic whirring sound as it charged up, preparing to deliver its sting. It was best that Stansfield didn't know how he was about to clear the tech area. The Admiral might not have been so glib about the device that was lodged in his head.

"Tweak the focus, broaden the delivery area," muttered Hunter as he reconfigured fiddled with the configuration of his arm, "and here we go." He triggered the microwave laser in his arm and directed a wide burst at the massive nest of OctoBots. Nothing happened at first, but then they stirred as the blast took effect.

Safe behind his mesh, Hunter played the beam across the Octo-Bots, guided by the targeting matrix in his HUD. As each OctoBot was struck, their humanoid brains quickly began to sizzle as the microwaves boiled them alive. In seconds, the translucent carriers cracked like eggs falling to the floor.

The OctoBots fell and danced, desperate to escape the searing heat, but all were caught. Hunter swept his hand back and forth, targeting everything he could see until the air was sharp with the tang of cooked meat and nothing lived or moved in the room.

"Sautéed brains, anyone?" asked Hunter with a smirk. "I reckon I just solved your OctoBot issue."

"Are you sure you got them all?" asked Stansfield.

"Pretty sure, sir," said Hunter as he looked over the piles of steaming corpses. "I'm going deeper in now. I can see why you've been experiencing technical disruption, there's a whole load of cables that are going to need plugging in. Can you send me schematics? I'll have this fixed in no time."

"Give me a few minutes," said Yau.

While Hunter waited, he reset the laser's configuration to the default narrow focus, then he leaned back against the wall and stretched.

"No time like the present," he muttered, muting all his channels and leading back against the wall. He flicked into his arm's management system and delved into a little-used medical menu. "Where are you hiding?" he muttered as the options rolled across his HUD. "Got you," he said, flicking into a tool called *Internal Nano-Diagnostics*.

He browsed through the settings, not really sure whether his changes were making things better.

"Fuck it," he murmured, "might as well give it a go." He held the middle finger of his cybernetic arm to the corner of his right eye, took a deep breath, and triggered the tool.

There was a tiny snick as the tool went to work, then a sudden stab of cold as it injected nano-filaments through his tear ducts.

"Oh, that's weird," whispered Hunter. Lights flashed before his eye, like he'd been smacked in the head, as the filaments wormed their way into his brain. He fought the urge to blink and a swell of nausea. Updates scrolled across his HUD; *brain function normal* they said, then *minor nerve damage – repairing*. A counter ticked up as the tool continued to dig through his brain.

"Come on," he hissed, holding as still as he could, his good eye flicking between the updates and the world outside, "come on!"

A new message appeared – *foreign body detected* – and Hunter clenched his fist in a brief celebration. *Neutralising*, the tool reported. A few seconds later, the filaments began to withdraw.

Investigation complete. Foreign body neutralised.

Hunter let his arm fall away and relaxed, feeling truly free for the first time since joining the mission. He dabbed gently at his eye and grinned.

"Your move, Stansfield," he muttered under his breath. "Try to blow my head off and you'll get the surprise of your life."

A channel pinged in his HUD as a file was delivered. "That's the schematics, Hunter," said Yau, "and there's an engineering team on the way to assist. We'll get these systems back online and find out what's waiting out there in space."

"That's the safety overridden," said Wilkins, standing up. The crate of sonic disruptors sat on the floor in front of him, the lid off so that all the devices were visible, their red indicator lights winking. The disruptors were metallic spheres about the size of a melon and punched all over with little holes.

"We're ready to open the doors," said Commander Vernon. "Just waiting for the all clear from Mason; then we'll go in once the clone conduits are clear."

"Almost done," said Mason. "Give me a hand with this," he said to Wilkins. Together they lifted the crate, and then Mason nodded. "Open the door."

Marine Gibney triggered the control and the door slid open.

"In they go," said Mason as he and Wilkins heaved the crate into the bay. It bounced across the floor, spilling the disruptors as it went so that they rolled towards the monster Bot.

"And shut the door again," said Mason as he watched the spheres roll away. The doors slid closed, and he blew out a tense breath. "Three minutes till detonation."

"Standing by, Mason," Vernon responded. "We'll enter the cloning bay on your mark."

"Activating now," said Mason, triggering the five-second countdown on the disruptors. "Expect a surge in the cloning bays when

that thing finally stops feeding off our data lines. Three, two, one."
Even on the far side of the door, they heard the noise, or rather felt it.
The deep vibrations seemed to reach out of the bay and into the
chests of the waiting Marines and engineers, rattling their ribcages.
The high frequencies sounded like a squadron of demented mosqui-
toes, all chasing the last human on earth.

"Fuck, that's loud," said Wilkins. "Must be bloody unbearable in
there."

"Sounds like my kids on a holiday," muttered Gibney.

"Patch us through to the cameras," said Mason. Wilkins fiddled
with his data slate for a moment, then held it up.

"That is one unhappy Bot-monster," said Wilkins with a grin as
the thing charged around the bay, searching for a way out. "It's just as
you said. The thing's disconnected from our lines and it's going spare
in there. How long now?"

"At that size and weight, we'll give it another thirty seconds," said
Mason. "I want to make sure we've cooked it good and proper."

On the screen, the Bot-monster slammed into a wall, then took a
few staggering steps and collapsed on the floor.

"Looks like we've got it, Admiral," said Mason. "The MegaBot is
down for the count."

"Get in there, Vernon," Stansfield said. "I want to be sure we're
growing ourselves some nice new clones."

Wilkins killed the disruptors, and the corridor outside the bay
was suddenly quiet. The doors on the far side slid open, and
Commander Vernon and his small team stepped through into the
bay. As they moved cautiously around the room, inspecting the bots,
the lids of the pods began to move slowly upwards.

"The pods are opening," said Vernon, sounding unsure. "Is that
supposed to happen?"

"No, sir," said Taylor, the cloning expert left behind by *Colossus* to
assist with the deployment. "The clones won't be fully baked yet.
Mason, did something get damaged at your end?"

"Nope," said Mason. "The MegaBot released its hold on the
conduit lines the moment we started the blast. There was no explo-

sion, no damage. Just a lot of noise, and the clones should have been partially shielded inside their pods."

Vernon watched as the lids rose, and environmental control gases cleared from each unit. The bay had been lashed up by the *Colossus* crew in haste and hadn't yet been made ready to begin operating. *Vengeance* had replenished her crew from *Colossus* – before it was destroyed.

"What the hell is going on, Taylor? Is this right?"

"No, sir," said Taylor, drawing his pistol with a shaking hand, "this isn't right at all."

7

The information that reached *Vengeance*'s bridge from the cloning bay was confused and sporadic. There were screams, shots, and above it all terrifying, primal roars that brought a chilled silence to the crew.

"Dispatch security teams to the cloning bay," said Stansfield, casting around for Commander Vernon before remembering he was already in the bay. "Hunter, Kearney, get your teams over there immediately!"

He opened a direct channel to Vernon. "Ed, what's going on down there?"

There was no response. Vernon's comms were dead. Taylor's life signs were showing that he was deceased. Bygraves and Gittens, the accompanying security team, also showed no life signs.

"Mason, get in there," snapped Stansfield.

"Moving now, sir," said Mason. "Entry in thirty seconds."

"We're almost there," said Kearney, "we'll follow you in. What're we dealing with?"

"No solid information," said Yau. "Cameras are out, intermittent audio only. Proceed with extreme caution, we don't know what's going on down there."

"Acknowledged," said Kearney. "Where are you, Hunter? We could do with your help."

"We're on our way," said Hunter. "I hope you don't mind that I'm not dressed for the occasion, I'm a bit splashed with OctoBot brains."

"We won't judge you, Hunter," Mason replied, "but do make some effort to observe the dress code next time."

"Get me visuals in that bay, Lieutenant," said Stansfield. "I want to see what we're dealing with."

"Working on it, sir," said Yau, "but it'll take a while."

Once again, across the open channel came the screams of the small security team dispatched to check the area. There were shots in the background, and the deep, terrible growls of a beast.

"I want all teams to secure a wide perimeter around the cloning bay, but I only want Charlie Team going in there," said Stansfield as he considered his next move. "Charlie Team, use whatever force is necessary to rectify the situation. Extract Commander Vernon and his team. Destroy the threat to my ship."

Kearney and the remnants of her team clattered down the corridor, the lamps from the Marines' helmets bobbing through the shadows as they ran. They reached Mason's position at the same time that Hunter and his crew arrived from the opposite direction.

"Nicely timed," said Mason as he checked his weapons. In their power armour, he and his team looked out of proportion in the battleship's cramped corridors.

"We've got flame-throwers and pistols," said Kearney as Sanders, Leman, Crank and Stewart crowded in behind her. Compared to the armoured Marines, Kearney looked positively puny in her sweat-drenched combat fatigues. "Can we mix and match from what your teams are carrying?" Kearney asked the security lead, whose people had come well-tooled for the confrontation.

"Help yourselves," came the reply. "Rather you than me going in there."

"It's what we do," Hunter responded, slamming a new power pack into his cybernetic arm. "I'm guessing these things are organic rather than mechanical, if they've come out of the cloning bay. I'm opting for chest or head shots. Microwave laser," he said, raising his arm, "will blow a big hole in anything that moves."

"Just make sure you shoot the right thing," said Mason as he raised his rifle and stepped toward the door. He glanced over his shoulder at the team. "Ready?"

"Almost," said Hunter, taking a knife and handgun. "We may get caught in more close combat. I'd better have a back-up for the arm."

"Okay, everybody, let's go in and see what we're dealing with," said Kearney, adjusting her HUD.

"I wish they'd get the lights fixed," said Mason. "It's a bit shadowy down here, and I'd like to see what's in there before it finds us." He looked around at the Marines. "Everyone in armour follows us in. The rest of you hold position here, and if anything non-human comes out that door, shoot it in the face until it's dead, okay?"

There was a round of grim nods from the team as they prepared themselves. Then Mason nodded at Wilkins.

The door slid open. Beyond, the bay was dark and quiet. Even the familiar rumble of the ship's systems seemed dulled somehow. Thin wisps of smoke clung to the ceiling and wrapped their way around the equipment, flashing white as the team's lamps played across them.

Kearney, Hunter and Mason made their way to the top of the long corridor that led to the cloning bay, moving silently and with extreme caution. The Marines followed, working in pairs to watch every surface.

At the corner, Hunter held up his hand to Kearney and Mason, indicating that they should prepare to give him cover as he went ahead.

Then he darted around the corner, sticking close to the wall. Kearney sprang out from the corridor behind to protect him, and

Mason went back to back with her to provide cover along the corridor leading to the cloning bay entrance.

"What the hell did that?" said Mason, disgusted.

"Report, please," came Stansfield's voice, ever alert.

"It's Taylor's head," said Kearney. "It's been ripped off. What the fuck kind of creature can do that?"

Hunter surveyed the scene. "The rest of his body has just been thrown away at the end of the corridor. He looks like he was savaged; this hasn't been done with weapons." Behind him, there was a nervous shuffle as the Marines unconsciously closed ranks.

"Any sign of Commander Vernon?" Stansfield asked.

"Not yet," said Kearney. "We're moving on."

Silently, stealthily, the three elite troopers moved up the corridor. As the entrance came into view, they could see that there was an arm lying in the doorway. It was still clasping a handgun.

"Anybody see an infra-red signature?" asked Mason. "I'm getting nothing but background and equipment radiation."

"Nothing," said Kearney. "Any progress on the lights?"

"Maintenance teams report we're almost there," came Yau's reassuring voice. "It'll be only a few more minutes."

"We might not like what we see when the lights go on," warned Kearney.

"Wouldn't be the first time that's happened to me," said Hunter wryly.

The three troopers were now outside the wide entrance to the cloning bay. Hunter had gone to the far side of the doorway; Kearney and Mason had stayed on the near side, with the Marines spreading out to secure the area.

Hunter looked ahead. "There's another body further along the corridor. We have to consider the possibility that these things may be elsewhere on the ship."

"We've had no further reports," said Stansfield, "and nothing's shown up in the areas where the internal cameras are still working. We believe the perimeter is secure. Let's find out what we've been baking down there."

"On my signal, we move in," said Kearney. "Stay tight, don't get killed."

Mason nodded, mostly hidden in the shadows; then Kearney gave the signal and the door slid open. She and Hunter took left and right, moving directly for the cover of two control units. Light from the open lids of the cloning pods made the room brighter than the corridor, but that just meant there were more shadows.

"Best light we've had for hours," muttered Mason. Behind him the doors slid closed, leaving the three troopers alone in the bay.

Hunter was intent on something. "I can see heat signatures all around this area, but only one looks human."

"I'm not seeing anything on my HUD," said Kearney, frowning over her rifle as she panned the room. "How are you doing that?"

"I've got some more advanced kit built into my eye socket. It's nano-tech, much more effective than that crap Sol gives you."

Mason and Kearney exchanged doubtful glances.

"Are you serious?" said Mason.

"Sure," said Hunter. "Worth its weight in gold."

"I might try and get me a robo-refit one of these days," mused Kearney.

"You might want to reconsider that lifestyle choice, Kearney. This kit is neat, but you've seen how Sol responded. I get to spend my life as a Penal Marine, or they kill me. Either way, I'm a dead man walking."

"Yeah, maybe you're right," said Kearney with a shudder. Then she shook her head. "Just tell me what's fucking out there."

The cloning bay was the size of a small hangar. It was lined with banks of pods and electrical equipment. Stansfield had got the *Colossus* crew to install the kit they'd delivered, but there hadn't been time to deploy clones before the battle with the Firewall Sphere had begun. Being an older ship, *Vengeance* had needed more retrofitting to handle the data required for cloning, work that went beyond the quick fix Davies had rigged up.

"Something's moving," said Hunter, staring across the bay.

There was a roar from either side of the hangar, deep and

menacing in the shadows. Then two heavy, dark objects charged out of the gloom, screeching like wild animals.

"Fuck," said Kearney. "Who let the dogs out? Look at the speed of those things. Mason, incoming!"

Mason spun around as Hunter and Kearney opened fire. The crack of Kearney's rifle drowned out the near-silent hum of Hunter's arm-mounted laser, but the effects were clear. Both creatures collapsed to the floor, but their speed was so great they continued to slide towards Mason, who braced himself for the impact. He was slammed against the door by one of the huge bodies, pinned there with his feet off the ground.

"Good doggie," he murmured, reaching out to pat the ruined remains of the monster's head. "This thing stinks. I'm gonna need your help to get it off me, I'm completely trapped."

Kearney stepped closer to the corpse and began to sling her rifle. Then there was a growl in the shadows and she froze, staring briefly at Mason before she spun round to face whatever was out there.

"I see traces of at least eleven more of those creatures," said Hunter. "They're all over the place."

"What do you see? We're getting poor-quality images from your HUDs." Stansfield's voice was heavy with impatience and frustration.

"It's biological, whatever it is," said Mason, struggling to catch a full breath. "You should see the teeth in this thing. Its mouth has been half blown off by Hunter's shot, but it has a ferocious jaw. That thing could take off a limb."

"They're fast, too," said Kearney. "Imagine something heavy and wild like a bear running at you. That's what it's like."

"Are they human, mechanical, or something else?" Stansfield asked.

"More human than anything," said Mason. "They have legs, arms, a head, a jaw. I'm trying to get a good look, but I don't see eyes or a nose. They're like some half-formed or deformed clone. The best way I can describe them is that it's like they're unborn, premature. Like they came out too early, or maybe the cloning process got screwed with."

"I count twenty of those things in here with us," said Hunter, "including the two dead ones. Twenty. That's the number of OctoBots that merged in the vent. Remember Mason said they were all hooked into the conduit cabling? What if they sabotaged twenty of the pods and this is what came out? We interrupted them halfway through whatever it was they were doing, and this is the half-baked result."

"The numbers are compelling," said Stansfield. "It's too much of a coincidence. The Unborn theory makes sense too."

"There are things moving in the shadows," said Kearney. "We need to go."

"I've got movement," said Hunter. "They're heading for the doors and whoever it is over the far side of the bay."

8

"It's got to be Commander Vernon," said Stansfield.

"Well, he's completely outnumbered if it is," said Hunter. "Eeny, meeny, miny, moe ... towards which person will I go?"

"You go for the officer," Mason chided. "I'll figure my own way out of this little dilemma. You and Kearney see if that's Vernon, and get his arse out of there."

"You sure?" said Kearney doubtfully, although she knew the answer already. Commander Vernon came first. All life wasn't equal on a battlefield.

Mason nodded, peering out from his helmet. "Lend me a blade, though. Can't reach mine."

Kearney tossed him her knife. "Good luck."

"Okay, Kearney, we need to spread out wide, circle in on them from behind. Ready?"

Kearney nodded and readied her weapon. She'd fired on the beasts when they'd charged at Mason, but she had no idea if her shots had had any effect. Hunter had got straight in there with his magic robo-arm and taken them down, a single shot to each.

"Lights on in two minutes," said Yau over the shared channel.

"Maintenance team has found the problem and are just about to flick the switch."

Hunter and Kearney moved out wide, making hand gestures to each other across the bay until they both found cover.

"The objective is to get Vernon out, not kill the beasties," said Kearney. "You provide the cover and distraction, I'll find Vernon."

"Go now or they'll be right on him," said Hunter. "I can't believe they haven't found him yet."

He monitored the movement across the bay. There was a single human crouched behind a pod – Commander Vernon, probably – but a dozen or more other shapes were circling close around him.

"Vernon must have nerves of steel," muttered Hunter as he watched.

"I'm ready," said Kearney. "Moving now."

Hunter opened fire on the closest of the Unborn, both with his handgun and with the microwave laser in his cybernetic arm. The effect was immediate. From around the bay, the Unborn roared and scattered, some taking cover and others charging towards Hunter.

Kearney, weapon at the ready, ran towards the pod where Vernon was concealed and slid down into cover beside him.

"Are you alright, sir?" she asked, peering out to watch as the Unborn disappeared into the shadows.

"Throw away your guns, that's how they find you," hissed Vernon. He was holding his arm, his uniform was torn and bloody, and it looked like he'd lost his HUD.

"Are you wounded, sir?"

"It's just a tear, it'll stitch. But the guns," hissed Vernon, "they can sense them firing, somehow. Warn the others."

"Hunter, did you get that? The commander is safe, but he says the Unborn can sense gunfire."

"They hear gunfire and they're drawn to it?" asked Hunter, but Vernon shook his head.

"They're deaf," said the commander, calling across the bay. "But somehow they sense the discharges from our weapons."

"Fuck," said Hunter. "The pistol wasn't stopping them anyway. I've put two more down with the m-laser, but now I'm out of power."

There was a hum, and suddenly the lamps came back on. For a moment their eyes reeled from the brightness, having adjusted to the semi-dark of the emergency back-ups.

"Shit," said Hunter as he stared around. He'd known they were there, but it felt unnatural to be surrounded by enemies, even if they didn't seem to know where he was.

"Keep still," said Kearney, "you're surrounded."

"Yeah, I'd noticed."

"It's okay, I think they're blind as well as deaf," said Vernon.

"Damn, these things are ugly," said Hunter. He stood perfectly still, relieved that the sound of his voice didn't draw any attention but not liking the way the Unborn were thrashing around. Their long limbs swept back and forth, as if groping the air for something.

"I think they're hunting me," he said quietly, backing away.

"What are you looking at?" came Stansfield's voice.

"They're like half-formed humans, sir," said Hunter. "Nasty ones, just blobs of flesh with long legs and arms. No eyes, no ears, no nose, but a terrible set of teeth. Can't tell if they're male or female. Unborn is the perfect description; they're alive, but they're not all there. I reckon I might've dated one of them."

"Any sign of intelligence?" asked Stansfield, eager to assess the risk to the ship.

"They're pretty fucking savage," murmured Hunter as he moved past a bank of equipment, "but it doesn't look like the OctoBots managed to move their brains over. I wonder if that was what they were doing–trying to inhabit human forms?"

"The Mechs we fought in the landing bay were harvesting body parts," said Mason. "It's like they're hungry for flesh. Not to eat it, but to inhabit it. It's spooky as hell, if you ask me."

"I need to speak to Commander Vernon," said Stansfield.

"Sir," said Kearney, switching her HUD to public mode. "Go ahead."

"Pleased you made it, Ed," said Stansfield. "What's your assessment? Bearing in mind what we know."

Vernon nodded, but Kearney frowned, having no idea what Stansfield was referring to.

"Hunter's right, they're after human bodies or spare parts. These things–Unborn or abominations, whatever they are–they're cloning gone wrong. Taylor was the expert. We'll need help from the Admiralty if we can't re-deploy him, but I'd say these were half-baked clones. I have no idea where the teeth came from, unless the Bots were messing with the sequencing, trying to manipulate the cloning protocols."

"Manipulate the cloning protocols?" said Stansfield. "This just keeps getting better. Are you certain it's the weapons that draw them?"

"Yes, sir. It might be the Sol enabler units that are fitted in each device. I can't think how else they'd be able to detect anything, but whatever it is, it drives them berserk."

"Maybe that means they can sense my arm," said Hunter, trying to work out how he was getting out of his current position without walking directly into the path of one of the Unborn.

"Steady, Hunter," warned Stansfield.

"Don't do anything reckless," said Vernon from across the bay.

There was a tense pause.

"Seems they can't detect my arm," said Hunter smugly. "Guess that's why they didn't run for me when I fired at those two ugly mugs in the entrance. They must have locked onto the handgun when I was giving cover to Kearney. Hey, Mason, are you still stuck?"

"Yeah, it's not all fun and games," said Mason. The squelching sounds of a knife cutting bloody flesh floated across the bay.

"Are you actually cutting your way out of there?" asked Kearney with a disgusted tone.

"Yup! Remind me never to carve the Sunday roast ever again. These things are disgusting. I'll be with you in a moment."

"We need to lock the Unborn in here," said Vernon as he and Kearney edged towards Mason and the door. "They have to be contained. If they break out into the ship, they'll cause untold damage."

"Agreed," said Stansfield. "Can you get yourselves out of the cloning bay and lock them in? What's going on with the other clones we're growing? Are they alright still?"

"It's difficult to tell, sir," said Kearney, half crouching to get a better look at the pod she was hiding behind. "The lids are still down and the lights are on, I'm just not certain anyone is home."

"I've cut myself out," said Mason, a note of triumph in his voice. "I'm covered in blood and flesh, no need to tell me how nice I look next time you see me."

"So what's the plan?" asked Hunter, ignoring Mason. "Bearing in mind I'm standing here in the middle of these butt-ugly Unborn bastards, and not one of them has discovered mouth mints or breath freshener. They remind me of Ten!"

"What have you got hidden in that arm of yours?" asked Kearney.

"Microwave laser's the only ranged weapon, but it's a power-hungry bitch and I'm out. There's a blade, and a short-range mono-filament blaster if you've got the ammo, but that's about it."

"We weren't asking for a copy your arm's specs," interrupted Stansfield, angry and impatient.

"Apologies, Admiral. In short, I've got nothing. I'm a bit trapped here. I'm tempted to use a knife, try to take down as many as we can."

"I was thinking the same thing," said Mason.

"No," said Kearney sharply. "They're fast and dangerous, but they're dumb. We lock them in, formulate a plan, then come back and kill the lot of them."

"Seconded," said Vernon. "Everybody out, converge on Mason's position."

"Is that the best solution?" asked Stansfield.

"I had fifteen minutes to watch these things, sir," replied Vernon. "You won't believe the speed they move when they get a scent. One of them ripped Taylor's head straight off, like it was tearing the corner off a piece of paper..."

"Admiral, we have a problem." Yau's voice could be heard in the background, picked up by Stansfield's comms unit.

"One moment. Can you make this work, Ed?"

"I don't see there's any other choice, sir."

"Our teams are standing by in the corridor, sir," said Kearney. "These things are nasty, but against armoured Marines? No contest."

There was a pause in the discussion as Stansfield held a rapid argument with Lieutenant Yau, whose desire to interrupt seemed, to Kearney, to border on the suicidal.

But there was no mistaking Stansfield's tone a few moments later.

"We have another problem. Vernon, get up here immediately. Charlie Team, clear that bay. I want the cloning suite under our control and fully operational in an hour. Out."

"Admiral?" said Vernon, astonishment on his face. There was no reply. "He's cut the channel," he said, bewildered and a little discomfited.

"We'd better get you to the bridge, sir," said Kearney. "Then we can start cleaning up this mess."

9

I n his entire career in charge of a battleship, Stansfield had never missed a beat when it came to making a decision or choosing a course of action. But when he saw what was on the screen, he needed a few seconds before he could begin to comprehend its sheer scale.

"Distance, Mr Henry?" he asked after a few moments. The bridge crew were looking to him for a response.

"Just over a hundred and thirty light minutes, sir. They're heading in this direction and to this point in space. They're moving fast, too."

"If any of those battleships have weapons like the ones on the Sphere..." said Stansfield before falling silent. He shuddered at the thought of super-powered enemy battleships.

"I don't think they can have, sir," said Lieutenant Yau. "The records Hunter exfiltrated suggest the ship-killing weapon system on the Sphere requires its power management components to be arranged in a particular shape. My hypothesis is that this explains the unusual shape of the Spheres."

"Let's hope you're right, Lieutenant," said Stansfield sceptically, "because otherwise this will be the shortest engagement in history." He stared at the image for a little longer as he collected his thoughts. Then he nodded once, his decision made.

"Take it off the screen," he said firmly. "They're too far away to pose an immediate threat, whoever they are, and we have our own problems. Ed, I need you here by my side for this one, you're going to want to take a look at this."

"We're on our way, sir," said Vernon, "just weaving through this nest of Unborn bastards."

"Ten minutes, Commander." Then Stansfield closed the channel and sat back in his chair, deep in thought.

Kearney was keen to hear what had happened on the bridge. She sure as hell was getting out of the cloning bay alive–there was no way she was missing out on whatever had silenced Stansfield.

"We're going to start moving," said Mason. "Hold steady, Hunter, we'll prioritise getting you out of the middle of those things."

Mason approached from the front, knife at the ready. It suddenly seemed like a very small blade. "You sure about this?" he asked as Kearney and Vernon approached the pack of Unborn from the other side.

"No," said Kearney, "not really."

"Great," grunted Mason, edging forward. The Unborn had all quietened down, as if they were now safe from harm, but the air of menace was tangible.

But Charlie Team stayed silent, tense and on edge as soon as they moved within a metre of the beasts. Hunter was completely encircled. There was no way he was breaking out of that grouping without help. They all selected their first kill.

"That one," said Kearney, pointing at an Unborn, "and that one, then we run. On my move." The two Unborn she had chosen were between Hunter and the door. Kill them both, and they'd have a chance to escape.

"Go," she said, launching herself at one of the targets.

Hunter yelled as he thrust his knife into the head of the nearest Unborn. There was less resistance than he'd expected, and the powerful blow dropped the beast to the floor even as Mason stabbed it from behind.

Vernon and Kearney fell upon their target, slashing at its chest and head. The creature let out a deathly roar, and began to thrash and snap its teeth, wrenching around to snap at its attackers.

And then the whole bunch of them was moving. The wounded beast thrashed as if demented, its movements even more unpredictable than the others. Kearney was struck by a flailing limb and catapulted across the room. Mason slashed at another Unborn as he was thrown to the floor and trampled by two of the beasts, his armour creaking under their weight.

Vernon slashed and stabbed, screaming unheard abuse at the Unborn, his injured arm held tight across his chest. Hunter heaved Mason back to his feet.

"It's all gone to shit," Hunter yelled. "These things are too strong for knives to kill them."

"Move," shouted Mason as Vernon was struck by an Unborn as it raced past, mouth slobbering. The commander was knocked to his knees, momentarily dazed as his knife skittered away across the floor.

"Get to the doors," Hunter shouted, pushing past a corpse to look at the stunned commander. "Get to the doors. Mason, grenades!"

"Yeah, right," said Mason, snatching a pair of grenades from his pack and tossing them to Hunter. "You reckon they'll sense these as well?"

"I fucking hope so," said Hunter as he activated the grenades and threw them into the open space at the far end of the bay.

The grenades clattered and bounced across the bay's deck, and the Unborn ran after them like a pack of wolves falling on their prey.

"It's now or never," shouted Hunter, heaving the still-dazed Vernon to his feet and dragging him towards the door in a stumbling run. Behind them, the grenades went off one after another, blasting blood and muck across the bay.

"Wilkins, open the door," yelled Mason as he ran.

"Roger," said the tech. Moments later the door slid open,

revealing Wilkins and Leman in full power armour with weapons raised.

"No," shouted Kearney as she ran, "stand down."

But the Marines weren't focussed on Kearney. They were watching the horror unfolding in the bay as the Unborn milled around in search of their prey.

Wilkins sighted down the rifle and fired, a short, controlled burst at the nearest Unborn. It fell back, stung by the bullets, then let rip a scream of primal hatred. It turned to face Wilkins as the Marine fired again; then it charged forward, terrifyingly fast.

"Run," Kearney shouted across the bay as Leman and Wilkins fired again and again.

Vernon, still unsteady on his feet, stumbled into a run with Hunter at his side. Mason followed, putting his armoured bulk between the commander and the Unborn. Kearney dashed after them, stealing glances over her shoulder as she ran.

The Unborn were following, all of them. Their mouths were wide open, displaying razor-sharp teeth ready to tear through human flesh.

Leman stood to one side as Vernon and Hunter reached the door, slipping on the pile of guts that Mason had left behind as he'd cut himself free of the monsters. They charged through, and Mason quickly followed.

Leman fired again, taking a step back to ease himself out of the room. Wilkins slapped a fresh magazine into his rifle and emptied it into the nearest Unborn as Kearney skidded through the doorway.

"Shut it, shut it," she screamed as she slid across the deck on her back, scrabbling to regain her footing.

The Unborn screamed. The doors squealed through the blood, and then they clicked closed.

Moments later there were two dull bangs as the chasing Unborn hammered into the doors. In the corridor, Charlie Team and the Marines stood listening to the shrieks of the hideous creatures as they battered at the doors.

"They're locked, right?" said Kearney from her spot on the floor. She'd decided that standing up was too much effort.

"Right," said Wilkins, his rifle smoking gently at his side as he checked his data slate. "Yeah, locked."

"Thank fuck for that," whispered Kearney, laying her head back on the floor and closing her eyes.

"And the other doors?" said Vernon. Wilkins stared at him from within his helmet. "The other doors, Marine," hissed the commander, "at the other end of the bay."

There was a moment of appalled silence; then Wilkins stabbed at his slate, flicking through the other door controls.

"Closed and locked, sir," said Wilkins, holding up the slate as evidence.

"Did we get them all?" demanded Mason, his helmet off and his cool slipping away. "Are they all in there?"

Wilkins flicked again at his slate, searching for the camera feeds from inside the bay.

Then a shriek echoed down the corridor from a long way off, a terrible noise that reverberated through the ship and pulled at the nerves of the waiting Marines.

"I don't think they are," said Wilkins in a small voice. "The other doors were open, a few may have left."

"Fuck," said Hunter angrily, shaking his head.

Vernon stabbed a finger at the wall-mounted comms device. "Security teams, we have Unborn on the loose. Do not – repeat – do not fire your weapons at them. Let them pass."

Kearney's HUD, still set to public mode, suddenly came alive.

"Vernon?" Stansfield's voice. "Vernon, are you there?"

"Ay, sir, we're all here, but we've got Unborn loose in the ship. We're going to track them down and kill them before they do any more damage."

"Let Charlie Team handle that," said Stansfield, his voice unusually strained. "I need you on the bridge immediately. We have an armada of alien ships heading directly for us."

10

By the time Commander Vernon reached the bridge, it was completely silent. For a moment he wondered what had made things so unnaturally quiet, but then he saw what was on the screen.

The images were blurred by the vast distance and the impaired abilities of *Vengeance*'s ancient sensors, but even so it was clear that they were facing a huge number of ships, far too many to count by eye.

"What the hell?" whispered Vernon, unable to pull his eyes from the main screen, where the ships appeared to hang in space. "Are they ours?" he asked, although he already knew the answer.

"No," said Stansfield bitterly, "they're not ours. Human, almost certainly, but not ours. Not Deathless either."

"Another hostile faction?" breathed Vernon. "What are the odds?"

The ships weren't of Sol origin; that much was obvious. Thin though the information from *Vengeance*'s degraded sensors might be, it was enough to run a comparison against the records in the database. No matches.

"Can we make that clearer?" asked Vernon. Yau nodded, and a few moments later a blown-up image of one of the leading ships appeared on another screen.

"A battleship," said Stansfield. "Larger than *Vengeance*, much larger. And they have many such ships." He glanced at Vernon and frowned. The man was bruised, shaken and covered in the gore of the Unborn, but he was still on his feet, and in Stansfield's book, that was enough, particularly when facing an enemy as formidable as this one.

And there was no room for debate: the ship was definitely a warship. Heavily armoured, it had multiple gun turrets and what looked like powerful forward-facing torpedo banks.

"An offensive fleet, then," said Vernon. "Whoever they are, they're not here for exploration and trade."

"Full analysis, Lieutenant?" Stansfield asked after giving a nod to Vernon.

"They're not being stealthy," said Yau slowly as he thought through the implications. "We probably wouldn't have seen them if they weren't actively scanning us. As it is, we've no way of knowing how long they've been there."

"And from a military perspective," said Stansfield, a tremor of impatience in his tone. "What can you tell me that might be militarily interesting?"

There was a pause as Yau looked again at his screens. "They're not hiding, so they don't fear us. That suggests familiarity, maybe contempt."

Stansfield snorted.

"They're coming to this point. We can see at least forty-seven battleships," Yau went on, "and another eighty-three ships of other types, probably a mix of supply ships, smaller warships, medical and cloning vessels, fuel transports and troop carriers."

"A hundred and thirty ships?" hissed Stansfield, slightly awed despite his long experience.

"That we can see, sir," said Yau. Stansfield gave him a sharp glare. "If they're travelling in single file, or there're other fleets that aren't scanning us, or–"

"Okay, I get it," snapped Stansfield.

"That's a serious battle fleet," said Vernon. "They've got a lot of support ships with them. Wherever they're heading, they mean to be taken seriously."

"We know where they're heading," Stansfield said quietly to his second-in-command. "The only question is, will the Admiralty listen?"

Vernon frowned, but Stansfield had moved on to the next problem. "How long till they arrive?"

"If they mean to stop here," said Yau, "then about forty-eight hours. If not, maybe thirty hours or less."

"And they're heading for this location?" Vernon queried.

"Yes, sir, this precise point in space."

"They're heading for the portal," said Stansfield, giving voice to the obvious conclusion.

The bridge was silent once again. The crew tried to take in the enormity of the onrushing armada. The images peered down at them from the main viewing screen, taunting them with its dominance.

Stansfield roused himself. There was little point wasting time gawping at the bully in front of them. They needed to decide how and where to aim the punch to take him down.

"That gives us two days to prepare a greeting. How long till *Orion* joins us?"

"They'll arrive on the far side of the portal in less than an hour, sir," said Yau.

"Instruct them not to enter without my order," said Stansfield. "We don't want a repeat of last time. Do we have the Sphere team on the comms?"

"Patching you through now, sir," said Midshipman Khan, his fingers rushing over his console to link the admiral to Charlie Team.

"Conway, I need some results from the sphere. Either we incorporate it into our defensive capability, or we destroy it so it can't blast *Orion* out of space when she joins us on this side of the portal."

"Understood," said Conway. "We're making our way to the central control room, sir, and we'll let you know if we can turn this ship into anything useful."

"Keep me apprised," said Stansfield.

"What about us, sir?" said Kearney.

"Deal with the Unborn roaming our corridors and the OctoBots crowding our core," said Stansfield. "Until that job's done, everything else is at risk. I want drone cameras in the core so we know what they're doing there."

"Roger," said Kearney.

"Is there anything else you need?"

"No, sir, only time," said Kearney.

"Then snap to it. We have only forty-eight hours, and I want *Vengeance* to be fully battle-ready well before then. You have your orders, let's make it happen!"

Deep within the sphere, Davies was still jittery about OctoBots. Every creak, every movement within the structure put him on edge.

"It's all very well Stansfield issuing the orders," he griped, "but I'm struggling to get my head round this tech. It's almost human, but not quite Sol. It's like they've taken human tech and evolved it, but not in the way our tech has evolved. It's way more sophisticated than ours."

"Down," shouted Conway.

"Am I boring you?" asked Davies, absorbed by his examination of a console they'd found in a side room.

"OctoBot to your rear!"

Davies ducked into hiding as Conway fired. The bullets shot away five of the creature's legs, and the OctoBot was knocked off its perch on a bank of screens, narrowly missing Davies as it fell to the floor. Upside down, its remaining legs scrabbled at the deck as it tried to flip itself over.

Conway prepared to fire again.

"Whoa, steady," said Davies. "Let's take it alive."

"You sure?"

"Research," said Davies. "Need something to poke at if we're going to learn what makes it tick."

"Right," said Conway doubtfully, holstering her pistol. "But let's lose the legs," she went on, drawing her knife.

She sprang forward, pinning the OctoBot to the deck with one armoured fist while her other hand flashed, blade hacking quickly through the other limbs. Conway picked up the legless creature and peered at it. "Ugly little critter," she said. Then she tossed it across the room to Davies.

"Nice work!" Davies complemented. "Look, the brain's still active, only we've paralysed the little blighter. I'm going to see if I can interface with it in some way. If we can hack one of these things, it might give us some clues."

"It's all a bit geeky for me," said Conway as she sheathed her knife and unslung her rifle. "You need anything shooting, you call me, okay? The tech I'll leave to you."

"*Vengeance*, this is Davies, requesting permission for access to the ship's data files. Can you hop a link through my HUD, Lieutenant?"

"What's your thinking, Davies?" Stansfield interrupted.

"This thing has a human brain, sir, it's no alien. I want to know if I can identify it from its DNA. To do that, I have to access all Sol records. We might also be able to set up an interface to the Sphere; it's the only way we'll be able to make any sense of them."

"I advise deploying a local firewall, sir," said Yau, "and running everything in a locked-down sandbox. Then we can sever the link if anything untoward happens. I also recommend separate links, in a to-fro config. That way both links are isolated, and we can monitor activity on each line. If something tries to hijack one of the feeds, we'll know immediately and we can quarantine accordingly."

"Agreed. You'll have your feeds, Davies, as soon as Lieutenant Yau has configured the links. Work fast," said the Admiral, "because there's an enemy fleet inbound to our position."

"Thank you, sir, I'll be as quick as I can," said Davies. "Better get to work," he muttered. He muted the channel and stood back to look afresh at the part-disassembled console. Then, still muttering under his breath, he began to pull out cables.

Conway stood guard as Davies unpacked his hacking kit and

wormed his way into the Sphere's systems. It was like watching a master sculptor at work as he hacked beauty from a plain lump of marble, and it felt to Conway as if it might take almost as long.

"How long is this going to take?" she asked after about ten minutes.

"Almost done," said Davies. "Some of these cables use Sol-standard connectors. Look," he said, holding one up.

Conway pretended to inspect it, then grunted.

"The colour coding is new, and the layouts are unusual, but with this little beauty we should be able to open the backdoor." Davies plugged the cable into a slim metal box he'd brought from *Vengeance*. "Helps that *Vengeance* is as old as time, to be honest."

There was a little more fiddling, then Davies sat back.

"I'm in," he said as a display lit up on the console. "Hacked and cracked, with a wireless link to my HUD. You want to know how many Mechs are still in storage?"

The display flashed, and what looked suspiciously like a management dashboard appeared.

"Looks like two thousand and forty-eight pods in total, with all but a hundred and twenty-eight deployed. Hmm, not good. Could be nasty if they all woke up. Let's post a monitor on those pods to notify us if anything changes."

Conway watched in awed silence as Davies fiddled with the Sphere's controls, progressively locking things down.

"Davies," said Yau suddenly, "we have your links. Connection details coming to you now."

A package of information appeared in Davies's HUD, and he unmuted the channel. "Thank you, sir, patching in now." He muted the channel again and opened the file. He hummed as he worked, feeding the settings into the hacking box.

"*Et voilà*," he said. "It lives." On the display, a new screen of information appeared, this time in the familiar colours and layout of the Royal Navy.

"So, Conway, what do you want to know about *Vengeance*? We can see pretty much everything with this level of access."

"How old is Stansfield?" she asked, not even having to think about it. "Can you pull up his files?"

"Nah, the Admiral's files are locked," said Davies. "Personnel files are still restricted, but there should be a hidden area in here somewhere, if *Vengeance* adheres to tech protocols."

Davies resumed his humming as he delved into *Vengeance*'s files. Then he splashed a new page of information onto the screen and stood back.

"Well fuck me, look at this," he said, staring in astonishment.

"Yeah, it's a screen with lots of code on it. I've had more exciting days, Davies."

"It's only a bloody Tombstone!"

"Again, Davies, my face is blank. What does that mean?"

"It's like a ship's black box. It records everything that happens on *Vengeance*, all the commands and events. The protocol originated in the Twentieth Century in aeroplane technology, and it's one of those things that never changed. This is fascinating."

"Do tell," said Conway, intrigued now despite her usual cynicism.

"*Vengeance* has been here–on the other side of the portal–for fifty-three years. That must mean Stansfield and his crew were in stasis the whole time, just waiting for the portal to reopen. No wonder the old man looks so damn ill, he hasn't had any fresh air or sunshine for over half a century."

Davies flicked more screens of information onto the display. "It even has the official story recorded on here, the one we were all fed in the Academy. Officially MIA, unofficially sleeping in space."

"Bloody hell," said Conway, leaning forward to get a better look. "So they've known about this portal for years? What else have they been keeping from us?"

Davies played with the controls in his HUD, moving files around and hacking deeper into the system. There was a sound from outside the door and he looked round, distracted.

"Might be more Mechs," Conway said. "I'll check."

She followed her rifle cautiously around the corner, leaving Davies to continue his interrogation of the system.

"It's just Ten and the others," she said a few moments later, returning with the Marines.

Davies peered up at them, a grim expression on his face.

"What is it?" asked Ten. "You look like you're about to release the world's biggest fart."

"This is serious stuff," said Davies, shaking his head. "Staines wasn't entirely truthful when he sent us on this mission."

"An officer lied? Why am I not surprised?" said Jackson.

"What do you mean, 'lied'?" said Ten.

"Stansfield and Vernon know exactly what's coming in that armada of ships," said Davies quietly. "They've fought this enemy before."

11

"They've split up," said Kearney. She was watching the video feed from the drone that was following the pack of Unborn that had escaped from the cloning bay. "They're going to be a devil to catch."

"They're as stupid as they look," said Hunter dismissively, slamming a fresh power pack into his arm. "Together they're dangerous, but alone? We hunt them down, one at a time, and drop them."

"Microwave laser, right?" said Mason, nodding at Hunter's arm. "It stopped the Unborn dead in their tracks."

"Interfaces with my eye," said Hunter with a smug grin. "Auto-targeting system, hits anything I'm looking at," he said, peering meaningfully at Mason. "Never misses. Very good for hunting great blobs of alien flesh and taking them down with a single shot."

"Well, we're going to need it," said Mason as he reloaded his rifle. "Nothing else has had much effect on them."

Kearney started moving along the corridor, checking the drone's position. "There's at least one on this deck, but the others have gone down to Deck Four. Preferences?" she asked.

"Let's clear this deck first," said Mason, "then move down the ship. Any idea where they're going?"

"No," said Kearney, "but I wonder if one of them was wounded?"

She had a tracking app open in her HUD alongside the drone feed, but it was showing the location of only two of the Unborn. "It isn't showing on the tracker. If we get a report from the other teams, we can factor that in as we go along. You armed and ready, Hunter?"

"Ready to shoot my load at a moment's notice," said the Penal Marine.

"I think I'm going to be sick," muttered Kearney. "Just make sure you don't shoot your load too soon, okay?"

The corridors were now fully lit, but eerie in their silence. The crew of *Vengeance* had been placed on restricted movements while Charlie Team and their supporting Marines hunted the Unborn that roamed the ship. Personnel areas were on lockdown until the situation was resolved, which meant that *Vengeance* felt like a ghost ship.

And there were bodies everywhere. Every few metres they'd come across a pile of Mech parts or, worse, a human body that had been caught in the fighting. It reminded them that the mission imperative was to save lives, not just hunt down the creatures.

Kearney raised her hand. Hunter and Mason stopped behind her. "There's one up ahead," she whispered. "Mason, you're up in three."

"Roger," said Mason.

Kearney held up three fingers, dropping them one at a time, and on the final finger Mason slid out into the corridor. He fired on the beast with short, controlled bursts, luring it into an attack so that Hunter could take it out as it ran towards them.

Only the creature didn't do what they expected.

"Did you see that?" Mason asked breathlessly as the Unborn disappeared into another corridor.

"It was too fast," said Hunter, "didn't catch it."

"It's got a freaking OctoBot attached to its head," said Mason, playing back the video from his helmet cams. The images were small, but they showed the OctoBot's legs latched onto the Unborn's head. "And it was moving completely differently from in the cloning bay."

"You think it's been hijacked by an OctoBot?" asked Kearney.

"That's what it looked like to me," said Hunter. "We've seen some crazy shit from these things. I wouldn't put it past them."

"If that's what it's done," said Kearney, "we're now dealing with a massive, ugly brute with enough brain to be dangerous."

"You're reading my dating profile," said Hunter.

"Only thing missing is the bit about the robotic arse scratcher," said Mason. "Mustn't leave out your most charming feature now, eh?"

Then there was the sound of flesh on a steel plate. The three troopers looked at each other; then Mason eased himself to the corner and peered around.

He jerked quickly back. "It's got arms now, four of the bloody things."

"It's salvaged parts from the Mech bodies," Kearney said as she flicked into the corridor cam feeds.

"Like Mr Potato Head gone bad," snarled Hunter, trying to get a good look at what was approaching them along the corridor. "I'm still gonna take it out." He stepped into the corridor, then dived back into cover as the Unborn opened fire.

"You didn't mention guns," yelled Hunter over the racket as smoke and bullets filled the corridor.

"I said it was armed," said Mason, waving his rifle. "Arms!"

"Quit whining," Kearney shouted over the gunfire. "Mason, you got any explosive tricks up your sleeve?"

"I've got grenades if you want to tickle it," said Mason, "or shaped charges if you want a hole in the hull."

"If we could get close enough," said Kearney, making an obscene gesture. Then she shook her head. "Forget that. We'll do it old school."

"Shoot it in the face till it dies? On three?" said Mason.

"Too slow," said Hunter as the firing suddenly stopped. He launched himself into the corridor, arm swinging around to bring the laser to bear, but he'd estimated it badly. "Argh," he managed as the monster shoulder-barged him out of the way, then skidded into the wall at the end of the corridor.

Hunter rolled aside as the Unborn shook itself back to its feet. Mason was on one side of the fork in the corridor, Kearney on the other, with Hunter stumbling around between them.

The Unborn screamed and charged again, guns discarded and arms raised to slash, as if the impact with the wall had barely registered.

"Get down!" Hunter shouted as the creature hurled itself at Kearney, its speed and power formidable. The creature raged up the corridor as Kearney fired again and again. Then she was gone, disappearing beneath the Unborn's bulk in a tangle of limbs.

"Kearney!" screamed Mason, emptying his magazine into the Unborn.

"Fuck," said Hunter as the Unborn screamed again, its chest a bloody ruin. Then it charged again as Mason dropped his rifle and pulled a pistol.

"The OctoBot," yelled Hunter, "kill it!"

Mason nodded and took careful aim. His first shot missed, but the second hit the OctoBot. There was an immediate change as the creature released its eight mechanical arms and leapt from the Unborn to the floor. It scurried away, leaving a trail of fluids behind it.

The Unborn, lost without its controlling brain, slewed to a halt, screaming its rage and pain, any hint of intelligence lost. It peered down the corridor.

"Where's Kearney?" said Mason as he slid a new magazine into his pistol.

Then the Unborn screamed and charged.

"It's all yours," said Mason, ducking aside.

Hunter grunted and raised his arm, all the time watching the creature's teeth and assessing the range.

"Pop," he said quietly, firing one shot at the Unborn's head. A hole appeared in the creature's messed-up forehead, and the monster dropped to the floor, its momentum sliding it along the deck. Hunter took one step back, and the tip of the Unborn's head just touched his boot as it came to rest.

"Miscalculated," he said looking down. "By one step."

"Where's Kearney?" said Mason again, looking around as Hunter nudged the corpse with his toe.

"I'm over here," said Kearney as she pulled herself to her feet. She was on the far side of the corpse.

Hunter blinked in confusion. "How the fuck did you get over there?" he asked.

"School gymnastics champion," Kearney deflected, scooping her rifle from the deck. She looked down at the Unborn. "One down, two to go."

"Gymnastics, my arse," said a disgruntled Mason, but Kearney just shrugged.

"Did you see how it changed when the OctoBot buggered off?" said Kearney. "The moment it was gone, the Unborn lost all control. It turned back into a crazy beast."

Hunter grunted and stretched his neck. "Where's the next one?"

"Somewhere on Deck Four," said Kearney, checking her HUD. "And if the others have picked up OctoBots, we could have a real problem on our hands."

Hunter opened a channel to the bridge. "This is Hunter. One Unborn dead on Deck Three. We're heading to Deck Four now."

"Move faster," said Stansfield. "One of the Marine teams is in trouble."

"Roger," said Hunter, closing the channel.

The three Troopers ran for the nearest staircase, making their way down as fast as they could get there.

"Steady," warned Kearney, scanning the cam feeds in her HUD as they neared the door to Deck Four, "hostiles nearby."

Hunter grunted and yanked open the door. Even before he'd stepped through the doorway, a decapitated head flew down the corridor and bounced off his chest.

"Whoa," said Hunter, looking out into a scene of bloody desolation. He eased into the corridor, peering carefully around the door frame. An Unborn stood twenty metres away with a Marine's torso hanging from its mouth, pools of blood and gore covering the deck.

"Found one," whispered Hunter. "No OctoBot on its head. Looks like we're alone with it."

The creature raised its head, as if it were sniffing the air. Then it dropped the corpse and padded carefully towards the doorway.

Hunter calmly raised his arm and triggered the laser. Nothing happened.

"What are you waiting for?" hissed Kearney from the stairwell. "Fucking kill it already."

"Technical problem," said Hunter, banging his arm against the wall, as if that was ever going to make a difference.

But the Unborn snapped around, sightless face staring right at the door. Hunter banged his arm once more on the wall, and the Unborn screamed and charged.

"Shit!" said Hunter, stumbling quickly back into the stairwell and heaving on the door as the Unborn swept down the corridor.

"Close it," yelled Mason.

"What do you–" Hunter began angrily; then the Unborn shoved on the door and Hunter was flung aside. He bounced off the wall and slid to the deck, blood running from a head wound.

The Unborn roared and dived at Kearney as she fired her rifle at the beast. It swatted her weapon aside and grabbed her, scooping her up in its hand and raising her above its head. Kearney screamed, flailing at the beast's head. The Unborn roared, shaking the helpless Trooper.

Then there was an explosion of flesh and internal organs. The Unborn crumpled, and Kearney fell onto the hard metal of the staircase in a mess of organic gore.

"Fuck me, that was close," she whispered, wiping blood from her face and scouring the area for Mason and Hunter. Hunter was shaking his head behind the door, dazed and now covered in blood and muck.

But Mason just stepped down the stairs, a big smile on his face. His armour was only lightly spattered with blood.

"You've got some pretty neat tricks yourself, Mason," said Kearney. "How the hell did you manage that?"

"You gave me the idea, as it happened."

"You didn't?" said Kearney with a disgusted frown. Then she

glanced around at the steaming, smelly puddle of monster guts in which she sat.

"Yep," said Mason with a grin. "Grenade up its arsehole, worked a treat. At least I think it was its arsehole. For all I know, it might have been an ear."

12

"We're being hailed by *Orion*, Admiral," said Midshipman Khan on the bridge.

"Patch them through, Mr Khan," said Stansfield. With two of the escaped Unborn down, the Sphere almost totally under their control, and, finally, some back-up from Sol, he was hopeful that things might be about to improve.

A face that looked far too young for a captain's chair flashed onto Stansfield's screen. "Admiral Stansfield," he said in a tone that held confidence beyond the man's evident years, "it's a privilege, sir. I'm Captain Ryan, and *Orion* is at your disposal. How may we be of assistance?"

"It's good to have you out here with us, Captain. What do you know about our situation?"

"Bare bones only, sir. Admiral Staines said you'd share the details when we arrived."

"The situation is fluid," said Stansfield, signalling Lieutenant Yau, "and there are many gaps in our knowledge. We're sending the briefing package. Your eyes only for now, Captain."

"Understood." For a few moments, Ryan was distracted by the initial flood of information onto his screen, and Stansfield couldn't help but take a frisson of enjoyment as he watched the cocky expression on the captain's face dissolve into one of earnest concern.

"*Resolution* and *Conqueror* are on their way," said Stansfield, "but they'll arrive a little too late for the initial engagement."

"*Orion* had been ordered through the portal to join you now the Sphere's been disabled. The Admiralty are keen to learn more about the ships you've encountered."

"Negative, Captain. We cannot yet confirm that it's safe for you to cross the portal. We believe the Sphere targets ships with the new Sol signatures. *Vengeance* got through because we're old school."

"But the Sphere has been disabled, sir, hasn't it?" Ryan persisted. "My orders are to follow you through and lend whatever support we can. In light of the arrival of this" – he paused to look down at his screen – "this 'armada', there doesn't seem to be any time to waste."

"That's as maybe," growled Stansfield, "but there's still the problem of the portal's defenders."

"*Orion* uses a new drive system," said Ryan, clearly not willing to be deflected or intimidated by Stansfield's history. "It leaves virtually no trace. What happened with *Colossus* was unfortunate, but the Admiralty believes it was due to the design nature of its engine system."

"It was due to offensive action on the part of the Sphere," snapped Stansfield. "I have to advise against portal entry, regardless of the Admiralty's orders."

But Ryan shook his head. "My instructions are clear, sir, both with regards to *Orion* and to your orders."

"My orders?" hissed Stansfield.

"We're not reckless, sir," Ryan went on, ignoring Stansfield's growing anger. "*Orion* has some of the most advanced equipment available. We're despatching a simulation probe to imitate our engine signature and test the Sphere's capabilities. If all goes well, *Orion* will cross the portal."

Stansfield glanced at Vernon, who was standing to one side to listen to the conversation. The commander shrugged, as if to say 'the Admiralty will do what the Admiralty will do'.

"You must make your own decisions," said Stansfield eventually, "but the Admiralty are a long way away, Captain. I urge caution."

"Noted, Admiral," said Ryan, without a hint of acceptance of Stansfield's warnings. "We'll wait here and let you know as soon as we're clear for entry. I have an engineering team working on your shuttle rig. It's very clever, but we're re-routing it to a StaticBuoy to improve performance."

"What," said Stansfield carefully, "is a StaticBuoy?"

Ryan looked briefly surprised. "It's just a buoy that retains a fixed position in space. It's a little neater than your wreck of a shuttle and it won't go floating off in space, so you'll retain your comms system when the portal is open."

Stansfield nodded, unable to fault Ryan's decision. "Fair enough, Captain. Now, I must get back to the matter at hand. Keep me informed. Out." And he closed the channel before Ryan could protest or offer more unwanted advice.

Stansfield flicked at his slate, opening a new channel. "Davies," he barked, "what's going on over there?"

"We're working on the interface between the Bot brain and our database, sir. Every step is firewalled so they won't get into our systems."

"How long till you're finished?"

"Twenty minutes, no more."

"Good," said the admiral, nodding. "Report back as soon as you're done."

"Ay, sir," said Davies.

"Carry on," said Stansfield. "Out."

"The shuttle crews are stripping the armoury and salvaging some sample Mech discs," said Conway as she tried to figure out what Davies was doing. "When are you going to ask Stansfield what's going on?"

"Only when I can do it in private," muttered Davies. "Not a good topic to discuss with everyone on the bridge."

Conway nodded. Davies was often a little paranoid, but on this occasion his caution made good sense.

"Admirals don't like difficult questions," said Jackson, glancing across the room from the doorway where he watched for approaching Mechs and OctoBots. "Makes them uncomfortable."

"Fuck uncomfortable," snapped Conway. "What about all this" – she waved her hand at the Sphere – "is there to be comfortable about?"

Jackson shrugged inside his armour and turned back to the corridor. "Just saying," he muttered.

Then the OctoBot lit up as Davies plugged in a lead to the tech bay. "Gotcha," he said in quiet triumph. Then he turned to the others. "I think we have a right to know what's going on, don't you? Bearing in mind we're risking our heads out here. The minute I can get to *Orion*, I'm getting backed up in their cloning bay. This mission is already way too hazardous to risk a real life."

"Seconded," said Conway, "but Stansfield is a tough old bastard, and maybe there's an operational reason we're being kept on a tight leash."

"Hah! Yes, but," Davies began, then he stopped dead. "Fuck, I didn't think that would work quite so easily."

"What?" said Conway, frowning suspiciously. "And shouldn't Ten and Gray be back from their scouting expedition?"

Jackson nodded and eased into the corridor to check for the missing team members.

"This brain's still alive," said Davies. "I've got a DNA sample, we might be able to ID the owner when we're back on *Vengeance*."

"Can we communicate with it?" Conway asked.

"I don't see a mouth, do you?" Davies replied dismissively.

"It's obviously still sentient in some way. There has to be a way to communicate. If we could speak to it, we might be able to find out what they want."

"Very commendable and tree-hugging of you, but I suspect that kick-arse armada probably tells you all you need to know. It doesn't need a Doctor Doolittle to speak to this animal."

"I still think it's worth a try," persisted Conway. "Just–"

But then, without warning, the panels surrounding Conway and Davies lit up and started flashing.

"What's happening?" Conway asked.

"Not sure," said Davies, frowning at the panels. He unplugged the OctoBot, but the panels didn't stop flashing. "It's not this thing, it must be something external." He opened a channel to Lieutenant Yau. "We're seeing activity on the Sphere, *Vengeance*. Is anything happening out there?"

"*Orion*'s probe just came through the portal," said Yau, his voice unusually tense. "And four more Firewall Spheres just dropped out of hyperspace."

There was a moment of frozen silence as Davies frowned and stared at Conway.

"Four more Spheres?" he said quietly, not quite believing what he had heard. "Are you sure?"

"Of course I'm bloody sure, Trooper," snapped the Lieutenant in a most uncharacteristic display of nerves.

"But," said Davies with a frown, "why aren't they firing? On *Vengeance* or *Orion*'s probe?"

"Unknown," said Yau. "They're converging on your position. You have minutes, if that, before they reach you."

"Roger," said Davies. He closed the channel as the sound of running boots floated along the walkway.

Ten came around the corner, Gray just behind him. "We need to get out of here," he said, deadly serious.

"What did you see?" Conway asked.

"This sphere is jointed," said Ten. "It's the first chance I've had to take a proper look without some Mech trying to kill me. I wanted to take a closer look since I saw *Centurion* painted on one of the panels towards the top. This thing's built from multiple, massive sheets of metal, each one hinged, jointed and tethered by these weird piston-like cable things. Never seen anything like it. And the entire structure is wired up to this tech area."

"Okay, so it's clever stuff," said Davies, "but is there a point to this?"

"Yeah. It's all moving, like it's alive or something. The piston-things are bracing. The entire structure flexed a couple of moments ago."

"I thought we'd damaged this thing so much it couldn't act anymore?" said Gray, frowning at Conway. "And aren't you supposed to be hacking it?" she said, switching her gaze to Davies and glaring at him.

"I knew something like this would happen," said Jackson.

"Maybe it's a rescue attempt," said Davies, lost in thought.

"Rescue attempt?" said Ten. "What are you talking about?"

"Four more Spheres," said Davies. "No time to explain, but maybe they're here to support this one and join the armada."

There was a moment's silence. Then Jackson said, "I hate it when I'm right."

"We have to get back to *Vengeance*," said Ten.

But before they could move, the Sphere began to creak and groan, and the lights on the panels flashed again, faster now.

"*Vengeance*," said Davies, re-opening the channel, "what's the status of that probe?"

"The probe came through safely," said Yau, "and *Orion* is now preparing to follow."

"Not sure that's a good idea, sir," said Davies. "This Sphere is reconfiguring. Looks like the changes coincided with the arrival of *Orion*'s probe, so there's something still alive over here, something that's not under our control."

"All the spheres are changing," said Yau. "We're watching them re-form as they close on your position."

"What are you seeing, Marine X?" asked Stansfield.

"Not sure, Admiral," Ten replied. "But I'd say these things are about to transform into something completely different."

He'd barely finished his sentence when his suit sounded a pressure warning as the Sphere's internal atmosphere was sucked away. In seconds, a hard vacuum had enveloped the party. Then the panels of the sphere began to move around them.

"We need to get out of here," said Conway.

"Back to the shuttle," said Ten, leading the way.

"Pass me that thing, Davies," said Conway, pointing at the disabled OctoBot. "If it belonged to a human, there has to be a way to communicate with it. Maybe Fernandez and his team can rig something." She stuffed the legless Bot into her pack.

"Go," shouted Ten, ushering them out into the corridor. The roof had gone, and the walls were going as the party ran towards the landing platform.

"Bollocks, I didn't break the data link," said Davies, stopping suddenly in his tracks.

"Forget it," snapped Conway, "we can't go back. Move!" She waved at Davies and he followed, swearing under his breath as Ten led them back towards the bay.

But now the exterior panels of the sphere were opening, moving and reforming. The entire structure was shaking, and there were gaps in the hull through which large patches of star-scape were visible. The walkway began to vibrate violently; then it tilted, moving downward into a different position.

"Shit," said Davies angrily, "don't tell Stansfield. I'll cut it off from the ship. It's a bloody good job I firewalled the links."

"This thing is like some giant geometrical puzzle," said Gray as she snatched at a railing.

"Bleeding engineers," said Ten, "they have to fiddle with bloody everything."

"We're not going to make it to the bay," said Conway as the Sphere's movements and rearrangements grew. The gangway was now tilting so badly that they were in danger of sliding off.

"The discs," said Conway, gesturing wildly at a squadron of abandoned Mech transports, "get on the discs!"

Conway made a leap from the gangway, and the others quickly followed suit as the gangway finally split apart behind them.

"That was too close," said Ten as they hovered in a group while the internals of the Sphere shifted and crashed around them.

"We're trapped," said Jackson.

"Over there," said Gray, pointing at a new hold that had opened in the Sphere's hull. "We can get out that way, if we're quick."

But before she had travelled more than a few metres, the Sphere's hull shifted again and they were trapped, blocked in by the crashing metalwork and completely enclosed by the Sphere's massive frame.

13

"We're going to get crushed in here," said Jackson, and for once his pessimism seemed justified. "The whole damn structure is collapsing in on us, like some sort of evil origami."

Always happier in the company of a circuit board and soldering iron, Davies was beginning to feel the pressure of the situation. The others seemed entirely at home, but Davies was struggling, and Jackson's morose pronouncements weren't helping.

"Give it a rest," Davies said, his tone higher than usual. Conway shot him a glance, but locked away inside his armour, it was impossible to tell how he was doing. She switched to the team's health readouts in her HUD, and what she saw wasn't encouraging.

Then a series of huge metal plates swung past and repositioned themselves, further restricting the area the team were hiding in.

"It's not destroying itself," said Conway as the panels moved silently past in what she might have described as 'a ballet of steel' if she hadn't been so distracted by the situation. "It's reassembling itself, which means there must be a safe place to take refuge."

"Agreed," said Ten, "it's transforming into something new. If we head towards the power and control area over there," he said, pointing at a patch of light on the far side of the darkened volume, "that has to be safe, right?"

Davies was off before the others had even had time to register Ten's suggestion. His disc leaped forward, shooting through a small gap and weaving its way back into the part of the structure that they'd just come from.

"Ten's right," said Davies as he shot off. "Whatever this thing is doing, it won't destroy its own power source or control area."

"Whoa, Davies, slow down," said Gray as she struggled with her disc. She wasn't quick enough off the mark; Davies was away like a greyhound with its arse on fire.

"What's up, Gray?" Conway asked.

"That's what's up," said Gray, pointing at a pair of massive structural girders that were about to shut Davies into a gap from which he wouldn't be able to escape.

"Fuck," said Conway with a grimace. "Davies, get back here."

But Davies wasn't listening. His disc travelled on even when the rest of the team were shouting at him.

"What the hell is wrong with him?" said Ten on a private channel to Conway.

"He never was one for the heat of a crisis," Conway replied. "He'd be happier stuck in front of a computer interface all day."

"How'd he ever become a Marine, then?" said Ten.

"Oh, don't worry, he can find it when he has to. It's just that Davies' default mode is *shit bricks*. When he has absolutely no other choice but to get involved in a scrap, never fear, you'll find the Marine that's hidden deep inside him. I guess he just figures that when you have me, Mason and Kearney covering your back, why get your hands dirty if you don't have to?"

She flipped back to the team's channel and tried once more to attract Davies' attention.

"He's panicked," said Gray, "and he's about to get himself locked in there."

They watched from afar as Davies manoeuvred his Mech disc through a narrow gap that took him to the control and power areas.

Then a huge girder closed the entrance behind him, and he was stuck.

"Davies? Are you hearing me?" said Conway again, hoping that he might have calmed down a little now that he'd reached his target.

"Er, hey, guys," Davies said hesitantly, a mild hint of fear in his voice. "I'm stuck in here! Where the fuck are you? I thought you had my back!"

"We were hailing you, you dickhead," said Conway, "but you weren't listening to us." She was annoyed with him. She'd seen this kind of behaviour from him before, and it never ended well.

"We need to move," said Ten, still staring at the structure around them. "The best place to shoot for is over there. If you take a look at how it's transformed, there's another protected area in the centre. At least we won't get crushed in there."

Conway looked around at the location Ten had flagged in his HUD and nodded. "Move," she said, "now!"

They glided forwards, Gray moving confidently on her disc, the others floating less adroitly, some way back. Conway, for all that she was a natural flier, struggled to make the disc go where she wanted. She weaved around, colliding with the panels that still moved through the Sphere's interior.

Gray reached the designated 'safe spot' and jumped off the disc, letting it cruise away. She unslung her rifle and turned on the spot, searching for enemies as Ten and Jackson bobbed down to join her.

"Hurry it up, Conway," said Ten as he raised his rifle. "You're cutting it close."

"This bloody thing doesn't work properly," snarled Conway, leaning first left then right in her attempt to make the disc go in the right direction.

"Faster," said Ten, waving at her as if that was going to make any difference. Conway leaned forwards and suddenly the disc accelerated, blasting across the gap between the corporal and her team.

"Too fast," said Jackson as he scurried out of the way, "far too fast."

Then Conway was amongst them. She jumped from her disc as it flashed through the area, landing on her feet, then falling into a roll to bounce across the deck until she slid to a halt. The disc shot away, narrowly missing Gray before disappearing off into the distance.

Then the light disappeared as more panels moved into place, and the deck shuddered as they slid together.

"Are we trapped?" asked Jackson, the lamps on his helmet flicking on to illuminate the new room the team were in.

"No," said Ten calmly. "Consoles, workstations. And doors," he said, illuminating each item in turn. "We're fine."

"We're moving," said Conway as the floor lurched beneath them.

"That's not good," said Gray. "And I can still hear that pulsing, only it's louder now, like a heartbeat."

"*Vengeance*, are you still hearing us?" said Ten.

"Just about," said Yau's reassuring voice, "only the signal's intermittent and we're struggling to maintain contact."

"What's going on?" said Conway.

"You're not going to like this, Charlie Team," said Yau. "The spheres are changing, re-forming. We think they're merging into one giant structure. If you could see what we can see, it's like a giant spherical puzzle, but it looks like the parts will all slot together to create some kind of monster space station. I'm sending a feed to your HUDs."

"Well," said Gray as the rest of the team watched Yau's feed in awed silence, "the Mechs know how to build big."

Then the lights came on and the artificial gravity vanished. The team were suddenly floating freely through what seemed to be a control room of some sort.

"Are you okay, Davies?" said Conway when it became clear that there was no immediate danger.

There was no answer for a few moments; then he said, "I just hit my damn head on some metalwork. Have you lost gravity?"

"Yup, we're just floating around back here, trying to stay busy, watching out for Mechs."

"It's only a matter of time," said Jackson, "before they find us."

"Charlie Team," said Yau suddenly, his voice broken by the poor signal from *Vengeance*. "Things are taking an interesting turn. Get ready."

"What's happening, sir?" asked Conway.

"The spheres are reforming," said Yau in an amazed tone. "The five separate parts are coming together to create a new structure."

"I don't like the sound of that," said Ten. "Doesn't make a lot of sense."

"It all makes perfect sense from out here," said Yau. "It's amazing, a really stunning piece of engineering."

"You may want to dampen down the praise, Mr Yau," growled Stansfield as he joined the channel. "Something like that presents a formidable challenge, and you'd do well to remember that."

Yau was chastened, but undeterred. "Ay, sir. Charlie Team, if you're in the power and control areas, I'd say you're about to become part of a greater whole. Hang on in there, and keep us updated if there are any new developments. We've still got our own shit to deal with out here, I'm afraid."

The three Marines could sense that there was movement around them, but in their state of weightlessness, they were spared the crashing against metal walls they would otherwise have been treated to.

Then there was a solid, heavy thud that shook the entire structure. Three more thuds followed; then everything went still.

"Is that the–argh!" said Ten as the gravity was abruptly restored. The team crashed to the deck.

"Goddammit," snapped Ten angrily, "why the hell weren't we near the deck when they switched the gravity back on? That hurt!"

They all heaved themselves to their feet and checked the room, but they were still alone.

"Are you okay, Davies?" Conway asked.

"Yeah," said Davies, "and this is good, guys. Very good!"

"What are you seeing?" asked Stansfield, alert to any new possibility.

"I'm at the heart of a massive control area, sir," said Davies.

"Everything that we saw previously has fused in this new structure; it's a one-stop-shop now for a tech-head."

"The Spheres are still reconfiguring," said Stansfield, "but surely that means this new entity has five times the capacity?"

"Yes, Admiral, that's correct," said Davies. "But it also means we only have one structure to disable, rather than five."

"That's not much comfort, from where I'm sitting," said Stansfield.

"Is there any sign of it powering up, Admiral," said Ten, "or making any other changes?"

"Negative, Marine X, it's just sitting there at the moment. And that pulse that we're monitoring has got more persistent. Are you still hearing it in the sphere?"

"Loud and clear, sir," said Ten. "It's ramped up now the spheres have come together. Do we know what it is yet?"

"Negative," said Yau. "We're still working on it. It seems to be some kind of signal, but it's nothing we can decipher using our standard databases. There's no precedent for a sound like that."

"So what's the plan?" Conway asked. "Now that things have changed again, I mean."

"Liaise with Lieutenant Yau," said Stansfield, "and take control of the Sphere. Stansfield out."

The Admiral dropped out of the channel, and Conway exchanged meaningful glances with the rest of the team.

"Take control?" she breathed, shaking her head. "Any ideas?"

"I'm going to work on the control panels," said Davies. "If I can hack into its central system, maybe we'll have some options."

"I'm gonna explore," said Ten. "And keep an eye on the Mechs, especially now that the five Spheres have joined together."

"Agreed," said Conway, "and take Jackson with you. Gray and I will try to find Davies and a way out. There's no point in Davies working his magic if we can't even find a key for the front door, and I'm guessing the shuttle is toast. Did you hear that, Davies?"

"Yeah, I heard. I'm located by the energy core. The control units have reassembled all around it now, so you shouldn't find it too difficult to locate me," said Davies. "It must all be joined up in some way."

Jackson strode over to the doorway and triggered the control. The door slid open, and he peered out into a long corridor.

"Death surely comes for us," he intoned as Ten joined him, "and yet what else is there to do but wait?"

"Yeah, I've got a few ideas about that," said Ten as the two Marines disappeared down the corridor.

Conway and Gray checked their weaponry; then they set off in the other direction, heading across a long, suspended walkway. The core was a hundred metres away, a giant structure that held all the important systems. And, somewhere, Davies.

"Lieutenant," said Conway, "can you get me a location for Davies? Any joy from his HUD, can you get a fix?"

"Checking for you now, Trooper," said Yau. There was a moment of silence, then, "I've sent a plan to your HUD. It's going to be a bit like hide and seek, I think. It's difficult to get a sense of the orientation."

"Thanks, sir, we'll take a look."

"Good. Let me know if– what the fuck is that?"

"Sir?" said Conway. The channel to the bridge was open, but the lieutenant wasn't answering.

"Lock down the bridge," shouted a voice in the background.

"Security to the bridge, Charlie Team to the bridge," said another.

Stansfield was issuing orders, but the entire bridge sounded like it was in a state of panic.

"Sir? What's going on? Sir?"

But from the bridge came only the sounds of gunfire and screaming.

14

"Bollocks, we're on the wrong level," said Kearney. "The Unborn's on the bridge!"

"How the fuck did it get there so quickly?" said Hunter as the team broke into a run.

"No idea," snapped Kearney. "They've summoned a security team, but we need to go."

Behind them, the Marines of their teams followed with weapons readied, all braced to deal with the final Unborn.

Lieutenant Yau joined the channel, his voice a whisper but his tone urgent and fearful. "This is like nothing we've seen so far," he hissed. Then there were screams, and then just silence.

"Sir, are you okay?" said Kearney as she slammed through a door into a stairwell. "What's going on?"

"Still here," said Yau, "but damn it, guys, get up here. This Unborn thing has an OctoBot on its head and another four around its chest. They've got needles stuck into it. It looks like somebody rolled their construction kit in a ball of dough! What a freak of a creature."

"What's it doing, sir?" said Kearney, trying to get the Lieutenant to focus as she sprinted up the stairs. There was only one thing worse than an Unborn roaming around the ship, and that was an Unborn with five OctoBot brains.

"It's trying to get to the main computer banks, we have only sidearms, and that thing's skin is so thick we're barely tickling it. It's killed Khan and Florence already."

"What about the admiral and Commander Vernon?" said Kearney. "Are they okay?"

"Yeah, they're holed up in the admiral's ready room. They got caught there when the creature came in. What's taking you so long?" Yau asked.

"We're using the stairs," said Kearney, "most of the elevators are still out. With you in a few minutes, sir. Stay safe!"

"Did you hear that, Hunter?" said Mason. "This is a hand job, and you've got permission to do it on duty."

"Very funny," snapped Hunter. "I hope Stansfield's keeping track of how much bloody trouble my so-called illegal arm has got us out of so far. If I wasn't such a generous soul, I'd have told him to get stuffed the minute he threatened to blow this thing in my head."

"He's softened already," Mason replied as they raced up the last flight of stairs. "His bark's worse than his bite. I've known people like him before. Once he knows he has your loyalty, he'll relax."

"But does he have your loyalty, Hunter?" Kearney asked.

"We're here," said Hunter, avoiding the question.

They jogged towards the bridge and into a scene of horror. A severed arm lay in the corridor outside the bridge, along with a head and a booted foot. It was like some awful version of Hansel and Gretel, with body parts instead of bread crumbs.

"Anyone you know?" asked Mason as they sidled closer to the doors.

"Thought it was Vernon," muttered Hunter, nodding at the foot, "but I think he was taller."

"Marine uniform," said Kearney, ignoring Hunter's joke. "They'd better have been clones. I hope we're not losing lives here."

"They still get to experience the death, even if they're clones," said Hunter. "They remember the pain if the backup works correctly."

"I know how it fucking works," snapped Kearney.

"I think I'd want a few memories erased if I got torn to pieces," said Mason, nudging the arm aside. "I don't fancy having my limbs ripped off."

"Better stay focused, then," said Kearney. She peered around the doorway into the bridge. Lieutenant Yau had taken cover behind his console, and he glanced over as Kearney gave him a nod to acknowledge they'd seen him. Yau's face was pale and splattered with blood, as was his uniform.

"Blood everywhere," muttered Kearney, scanning the bridge.

Yau's description had been correct; this Unborn wasn't one of the wild, bestial creatures they'd seen in the cloning bay. The OctoBots had hijacked the body, and this beast was altogether more intelligent. It still had its immense strength and ferocity, but this creature had a plan and a strategy.

"We're at a bit of a disadvantage," said Kearney. "All the entrances to the bridge are open after the last Mech attacks, so we can't corner it. We can't use Mason's explosive skills, or we'll damage critical equipment. Our only hope is if Hunter can get a clean shot to the head."

"And that still leaves us dealing with the OctoBots, right?" said Hunter. Kearney nodded.

"Is it trying to access the control area or the comms systems?" said Mason.

"I can't tell," replied Kearney. "Both, maybe?"

"That thing has five brains now," said Hunter as he powered up the microwave laser in his arm. "Hellfire, with an intellectual capacity like that it might even have a fucking clue how to complete a Sudoku puzzle!"

"Shit," said Mason as he checked his weapon again, "imagine a creature with the intelligence required to understand the offside rule. It would be an unbeatable enemy!"

Hunter laughed, but his humour died when there were shots fired by a Marine who'd managed to conceal herself on the bridge. The creature screamed and charged across the room. Before

Kearney could react, the Unborn had seized the Marine and pulled her body apart. Her still-screaming upper torso was flung out of the entrance where Charlie Team were taking cover, to bounce across the floor.

"Fuck, please let her be a clone," Mason said, unable to tear his eyes away from the Marine's tortured face.

"She's a clone," said Kearney grimly, putting a bullet through the Marine's head. "That's a modern uniform from *Colossus*, and they're all clones. *Vengeance*'s crew look like they missed a decade's worth of fashion supplements."

"Shit, we've got company," said Mason. With all the Marine resistance on the bridge now dealt with, the creature had sensed the shot in the corridor and was making its way towards them. And to get there, it was going to walk right past Yau.

Kearney mouthed at him from the entrance, and he mouthed back with what looked like an *Oh fuck!*

"Time to do your thing, Hunter!" said Kearney.

"Roger," said Hunter, nodding.

But the creature was too fast and too smart. It had spotted Yau, and it grabbed the lieutenant, picking him up with one arm. It roared at him and opened its massive jaws as Yau tried to prise himself out of the monster's hand.

"Hey, over here, fuckface!" yelled Hunter, stepping out in front of the creature with his arm set to fire. The creature roared and swung Yau around, blocking Hunter's shot.

Then Kearney appeared behind the beast. Hunter did a double-take trying to work out how the fuck she'd got there.

Kearney fired at the Unborn's back, her rifle on full auto as she blasted its armoured hide, emptying the magazine. The Unborn screamed as Kearney reloaded, still using Yau as a shield and swinging wildly around as it backed away from the two Troopers.

Kearney changed her strategy, aiming instead for the OctoBot clamped to the back of the Unborn's head. Her shots shattered the Bot's casing, and it detached itself and dropped to the ground, leaving a trail of fluids as it crawled away across the deck.

"This bloody thing is using Yau as cover for its head," said Hunter "I can't get a clear shot."

Yau screamed as the Unborn threw him around like a doll.

"I'm going for the admiral and Commander Vernon," said Mason. "I'm leaving the beast to you."

"That's right, Mason," said Hunter, "save the suits, don't mind me!"

"Er, it is actually military protocol, Hunter, but maybe you don't remember that bit of your oath?"

"Easy to forget the details sometimes," grunted Hunter, his pistol now in his other hand as he sought a way to free Yau.

The lieutenant still alive, but he was tiring fast. They'd not seen behaviour like this from the other Unborn. It wasn't using just anyone as a shield; it had chosen Yau deliberately, as if understanding that an officer might have more value alive than if it just tore out his neck.

Mason skirted the bridge towards the ready room as armoured Marines moved in behind Hunter and the Unborn backed away. Hunter had his weapon trained, waiting for a moment when the beast's head became exposed.

Then the creature suddenly switched tactics.

Two OctoBots, one from each side of the Unborn's head, detached themselves and jumped at Hunter. Primed to shoot at the monster, a straightforward attack was the last thing Hunter expected.

The OctoBots were clearly coordinating their actions. One clamped itself to Hunter's face and impaled him with its needles, paralysing him instantly. The other settled on his back and sank its needles into the flesh of his shoulders. Hunter screamed once; then he fell silent.

Kearney aimed, looking for a shot at the OctoBots, but she couldn't fire without hitting Hunter. Then there was a roar as the Unborn hurled Yau, sending him crashing into Kearney and knocking her to the ground.

The Unborn followed, charging across the bridge. It roared again, no longer concerned with human shields now that Hunter had been turned.

"Move," shouted Kearney as the Unborn stormed towards them. She pushed Yau away and heaved herself to her feet, firing three more shots. Her efforts had no observable effect on the raging mass of flesh and Bot; then its swinging fist smashed into her shoulder and hurled her back over a console.

The Unborn screamed and turned as Mason fired at it from across the bridge.

"Get up," he yelled at Kearney. Yau was with her, blood soaking his tunic as he tried to pull her upright. "Lead it away," shouted Mason, gesturing at an open door. He fired again as the creature charged.

"Shit," said Mason as he backed away, still firing.

But now Kearney was upright again, just, and she pulled out her pistol, wiping away the blood from a gash on her forehead.

"Over here," yelled Kearney, firing wildly at the beast's back. Her head was spinning so much she wasn't sure what she was hitting. Yau joined her, making as much noise as possible to attract the Unborn's attention.

The beast skidded to a halt, turned, and charged back at Kearney as she backed into the corridor.

"Hunter, some help," shouted Kearney as she retreated. But Hunter just stood there, as still as a statue, not even watching what was going on.

Then Kearney caught her boot on a corpse and fell back onto the deck. The Unborn screamed in triumph as it bore down on her, sweeping past Hunter as if he wasn't there. Mason fired again, stepping forward to place his armoured bulk closer to the beast as the Marines tried to herd it in from the other side of the bridge. Vernon joined him, retrieving a weapon from a dead Marine and sending a volley of rapid fire to infuriate the creature.

Stansfield ran to his command console and hailed *Orion*. The battleship might be stuck on the other side of the portal, but if they had any old craft on board, a rapid deployment of troops to *Vengeance* might turn the tide.

Hunter finally moved, taking a step towards Stansfield. His cybernetic arm came up, jerking as it moved, as if it wasn't under his full control.

"Take cover," yelled Vernon, pulling Stansfield to the deck behind the console. Hunter's microwave laser pulsed and sliced a hole through Stansfield's command chair, and into the deck beyond.

Then the Unborn screamed and charged across the bridge at Vernon. The commander fired again as he shielded Stansfield.

Hunter's arm flashed around until it pointed directly at Kearney, but the laser's power pack had been depleted and it did nothing more than click harmlessly.

The Unborn loomed over Vernon, smacked away his ineffective pistol, then grabbed him by the collar and pulled him to its chest. For a few seconds Vernon struggled against the Unborn's grip; then he screamed as he was absorbed into its body, unable to move or escape.

An OctoBot detached itself from the Unborn and scuttled quickly to clamp itself to Vernon's head. It released its needles and plunged them into the commander's skull.

Kearney screamed, and Mason raised his rifle, unsure what to do. Then Hunter brought his pistol up and fired. Bullets pinged from Mason's armour as Kearney and Yau dived for cover.

By the time they were back on their feet, Hunter and the beast had gone.

15

"What the fuck just happened?" asked Mason. He was standing at the edge of the bridge, staring around at the corpses as he reloaded his rifle.

"I'm not sure," said Lieutenant Yau, limping in from the corridor. He slumped down in a chair as Marine medics began to work their way through the injured. "I think Hunter's been hijacked by the Octo-Bots. They've overpowered his brain or something. As for Commander Vernon..." he paused, unable to find the words. He shrugged, then grimaced in pain and clutched at his ribs. "Looked like the Unborn subsumed him into its body," he managed.

Stansfield swept aside a medic as he crossed the bridge. "I'm fine," he growled, "see to the others." He looked around, face smeared with blood and uniform torn and dirty. "We've sustained heavy losses. I'm going to ask *Orion* to send a relief bridge team."

Yau could only nod as a medic lifted his arm and sprayed first antiseptic, then anaesthetic, then a thick layer of plasti-skin.

"You need to be in the infirmary," said the medic firmly, but Yau shook his head.

"Can't," he said, "need to be here."

The medic tutted and fussed, scanning Yau and shaking his head before uploading a short report and moving on.

"I'm pleased you made it, Lieutenant," said Stansfield to Yau, "but we need to get a grip on this disaster before it deteriorates further. What's your analysis of our exposure with Hunter and Vernon?"

"Too little data on Commander Vernon," said Yau, "but Hunter looks like a straightforward sequestration. The OctoBot is in control."

Stansfield grunted.

"Hunter could be a problem, sir," said Mason. "If the Bots gain access to his brain, they might learn things we don't want them to know."

Kearney was silent and thoughtful. She didn't want to make Hunter a target.

"Agreed," said Stansfield with a slow nod. "But he wasn't totally under their control. He hesitated, resisted, when the Bot tried to kill me."

"Did he, sir?" said Yau sceptically.

"Either way," Stansfield went on, "we have a literal kill switch. If Hunter is truly lost, we can take him out remotely."

Mason was shocked. "You wouldn't blow his head up, surely? Not after everything he's done for this crew."

"I'll remind you of your rank, Trooper. If you don't want to be cleaning out the shitters for the next week, I suggest you adopt the correct tone with your superior officers."

Mason realised he'd spoken out of turn and apologised.

"I think what Mason meant to say, Admiral," Kearney began, more diplomatically, "is that Hunter has already become a valuable member of our team. I know he's a Penal Marine, and I don't know what his crimes are, but Ten is a Penal Marine too, and they've both been invaluable to this mission. I'd respectfully ask that you don't rush to using that device on Hunter."

"Your sentiments are acknowledged, Trooper, but if I think that Hunter is a risk to my crew or my ship, I'll take his head off. Is that understood by everybody?" Stansfield looked around the remnants of

Charlie Team and his bridge crew. There were reluctant nods from Yau, Kearney and Mason.

"They also have Vernon," Stansfield went on, "and that's a different matter altogether. If the Bots get inside his head, they'll have access to an encyclopaedia of our operational secrets. That threatens not just our security, but the Admiralty's."

The team shuffled uncomfortably. What applied to Vernon applied to all of them, to some degree or another.

"Take whoever you need," Stansfield went on, turning to Kearney and Mason. "Use Marines, security teams, crew, anyone. Find Hunter and Commander Vernon. Get them back, but don't engage if it puts Vernon's life in danger. Is that clear? Then go."

Mason and Kearney acknowledged their orders and left the bridge, leading the remains of their Marine teams back into the ship.

"Lieutenant Yau," said Stansfield, "I need you here on the bridge. There'll be time for recovery later, but first we have to regroup and find out if *Orion* are still hell-bent on joining us at this side of the portal. Can you do that?"

Yau was bruised, bloodied and exhausted. His uniform was a torn mess, and his hand shook as he picked up a data slate from the floor of the bridge. But he nodded slowly and limped back to his post to begin the process of coordinating the fragmented teams on board the ship.

"Good man," said Stansfield. The admiral stood for a moment, staring at the neat hole Hunter's laser had burned in the command chair, then he shook his head and sat down.

"I have Captain Ryan, sir," said Yau, sounding about a thousand years old. "*Orion* is offering to deploy our backed-up people to new clones."

"Good," said Stansfield as he watched the first security detail arrive and begin clearing the deck of corpses.

Yau watched as colleagues he'd worked with for years were hauled unceremoniously from the deck. They'd been on many journeys together, lain asleep alongside each other in the stasis bays for over fifty years, yet they wouldn't have the privilege of returning to clone bodies like the crews of *Colossus* and *Orion*.

Yau took a deep, calming breath, and moved on, placing duty first. There would be time to mourn, but first they had to dispatch the enemy.

"Admiral Stansfield," said Captain Ryan, beaming down from the main screen and apparently oblivious to the damage sustained by *Vengeance*'s bridge. "I'm pleased to report that the simulation probe has completed its journey to your side of the portal, and all data indicates that we're clear to join you."

"We could certainly use some help, Captain."

"Marine reinforcements are on their way," Ryan went on, "and we're prepping a replacement bridge crew."

"They're familiar with our systems?"

"Somewhat," said Ryan, in a tone Stansfield took to mean 'no'. "The Admiralty asked us to prepare, but cross-training to *Vengeance*'s systems was a lower priority activity." He paused to cough, and his tone became more positive when he resumed. "Everybody we send you is riding a modern clone, so your risk profile should be lowered."

"I appreciate that, Captain. We've lost some good people on this ship. I wish we'd been afforded the luxury of cloning when *Vengeance* was fully operational."

"I do have one piece of news for you, which I'm passing to your secure line now. It's from the Admiralty, sir. They asked me to ensure that it was delivered personally."

Stansfield saw the data package arrive on his console; then he looked back at Ryan. "You're still on my screen, Captain. Is there anything else?"

Ryan looked briefly awkward before burying it beneath a veneer of professionalism. "The Admiralty requested I stay online to ensure that you'd received, read and acknowledged the order, sir. They said something about previous requests failing to reach you due to problems with the portal."

Stansfield snorted, certain that the Admiralty were far more aware of the reason behind *Vengeance*'s 'communication problems' than Ryan was letting on. He opened the data package and skimmed the contents, growing angrier the more he read.

"This is ridiculous," said Stansfield. "They want me to give Woodhall an executive command role? Do they know what a liability that man has been already?"

Ryan said nothing, waiting impassively as Stansfield read the rest of the brief note.

"And I'm to clear operational decisions with either you or Woodhall, eh?"

"Thank you, sir," said Ryan with a respectful nod. "I'll confirm to the Admiralty that you have received and understood the orders." The channel closed, and Ryan's face disappeared from the screen.

Stansfield's face was red. The Admiralty's orders were outrageous, but he hadn't risen to his current rank without learning to apply creative discretion.

"Get Woodhall up here," he said to the bridge in general.

"Ay, sir," said Yau, now playing multiple roles as one of the few officers left alive. "*Orion* confirms they're about to cross through the portal, sir."

"Good luck to them," muttered Stansfield. He stood up to head for his ready room, but Yau called him back.

"Sir," said Yau, and something about his tone gave Stansfield a bad feeling. "The armada, sir," he went on, flicking images onto the main screen. "They've split their force, and six battleships have jumped closer. Some sort of fast-flit hyperspace technology, maybe."

"Closer?" said Stansfield with a frown. "How long till they arrive?"

Yau looked up at the Admiral, and Stansfield saw the fear in his eyes. "No more than six hours, sir."

16

S tansfield could barely contain his anger with Woodhall. He'd attempted to keep matters civil, but it was soon apparent that his new executive officer had every intention of interfering.

"What news on the captured Mech, Lieutenant?" Stansfield had asked as soon as Woodhall had reached the ready room. "What do we have to report back to Sol so far?"

Woodhall ignored the question and sat, uninvited, in a chair across the desk. "I think we both know why I'm here, Admiral. Following my formal complaint to the Admiralty about your deliberate ignoring of the order not to enter the portal, I requested an intervention to help me contain your more maverick tendencies."

Stansfield took a deep breath, then an extra one just for good measure. He was too old to be throwing punches at arseholes, but Woodhall was sailing dangerously close to the rocks.

"Regardless of the Admiralty's orders," Stansfield said coldly, "I'm sure you'd agree that when it comes to matters in the field I am, perhaps, better placed to make strategic judgements."

"No, Admiral, I do not agree. And neither does the Admiralty," said Woodhall.

"*Colossus* would still be here if the Admiralty had followed my advice," Stansfield snarled.

"There is more going on here than meets the eye," said Woodhall. "You have not disclosed to the Admiralty all that you knew, and that lack of honesty has led both to the loss of *Colossus* and many deaths on *Vengeance*."

Stansfield narrowed his eyes and stared at Woodhall for a few seconds, then sat back in his chair.

"You're being deliberately obstructive, Admiral," Woodhall went on. "I'm sure we can agree that we both want the same thing. We need to deliver the correct result for Sol, we must defend and protect this portal and prevent whatever is approaching from passing through into our territory. And we have to do it all with very limited resources."

Stansfield cursed inwardly. Woodhall had done his conflict management training and gone straight for the jugular – common ground. What could Stansfield say to argue with that?

"Be that as it may," said Stansfield carefully, "we clearly need some rules of engagement to–"

"I'm not sure we do," said Woodhall, a sneer on his face, as if he sensed an advantage and was going to make full use of it. "It's quite clear in the guidelines. My executive command role requires you to run any and all strategic decisions or actions through me first. If I consider them to be contrary to the Admiralty's objectives, I may overrule or consult further with the Admiralty before they are implemented."

Woodhall stood up, apparently in an attempt to end the interview. "You've brought this upon yourself, Admiral, by stomping off into space to do as you please."

"With all due respect, we've delivered some impressive results in a short–"

But Woodhall interrupted again, "It was my actions that showed it was safe to go through the portal–"

"As as a result of your incompetence in our SEVs," snapped Stansfield. "Incompetence that could have resulted in the death of a valued member of the team."

"Marine X?" scoffed Woodhall. "He's a Penal Marine in a standard clone. He's entirely disposable–"

"And perhaps that's the difference between us, Lieutenant," said Stansfield, his sudden anger forcing him to his feet despite his exhaustion. "Clones or not, each life is equally valuable, and nobody is ever disposable."

An awkward silence hung in the air; then Woodhall cleared his throat.

"That is precisely why I'm needed here," said Woodhall. "The Admiralty needs to be certain that you have the right temperament to make difficult decisions," he went on as Stansfield boggled at him, "and to follow orders delivered within a legally mandated command structure."

Woodhall moved to leave, then turned back to Stansfield with a finger raised. "And I'll need a desk," he said, as if ordering coffee, "in here, so that we can work together. I take it you'll make the arrangements?"

Stansfield stared at him, unsure if his ears were working properly. "We're still clearing bodies off the bridge," he hissed, "and you want me to arrange a–"

Stansfield stopped himself. If he didn't manage this relationship, he'd be relieved of duty. He and Vernon both knew things that could tip the balance in this war, but they needed to keep their powder dry. This showdown could wait for another day. Besides, with Woodhall's expertise, it was highly likely the man would blunder into an airlock and shoot himself out into space before he had any serious decision-making to do.

Stansfield took a deep breath. "I'll arrange a desk," he said more calmly, "and we can work through our differences later." He'd done the conflict training too, albeit many years ago. He knew how it worked.

"Our priorities," said Stansfield before Woodhall could interrupt, "are to clear the ship of bodies, hunt down the remaining OctoBots, retrieve Commander Vernon from the clutches of the Unborn, and free Hunter from whatever has hijacked his brain. And we'll sort you out a desk."

"I suspect you're being facetious, Admiral," said Woodhall sternly, "but I'll overlook that for now. We should also take new crew on board when *Orion* arrives and beef up *Vengeance*'s defensive capabilities. In the meantime, I hope you don't mind me using your desk until mine arrives?"

Woodhall wiped his hand across the surface of Stansfield's desk and looked at his dust-caked hand in disgust.

"Be my guest," said Stansfield in disbelief, standing up to let Woodhall take his place. "I'll have some polish sent over straightaway."

Then he strode out of the ready room back onto the bridge. The last of the bodies was being cleared as he took his command chair. He would soon have his temporary bridge crew, and the ever-reliable Lieutenant Yau was present.

"Update me, please, Lieutenant. And get a desk and some polish for Lieutenant Woodhall in my ready room."

Yau nodded but asked no questions. The whole crew knew what *that* tone meant, and they stepped lightly around the admiral when he used it.

"Sir," he said instead, focusing on the task at hand. "Charlie Team are tracking Commander Vernon and Hunter. The new bridge crew will be here in less than twenty minutes. *Orion* is about to cross the portal. The team on the Battle Sphere hasn't yet reported in."

"The 'Battle Sphere'?"

"That's what we're calling it, sir," said Yau. "Let me pull it up on the main screen."

Stansfield looked at the image, and he had to agree that Yau was right. It looked exactly like something built to do battle, but it wasn't a perfect sphere. To Stansfield, it looked more like a mad steel-worker had blown five bubbles and mashed them together to form one giant body.

There were now gun turrets around the original five spheres, making the structure a formidable weapon. At five times the size of the smaller spheres, it was instantly more threatening and intimidating.

"Good name," muttered Stansfield, nodding slowly. "Contact Conway," he said, "and get an update on their progress. We need to know if that thing's an asset or a liability."

"Roger," said Yau, opening a channel.

Stansfield opened his own channel to *Orion*.

"Admiral," said Ryan. The man looked smug, and Stansfield guessed that he'd already spoken to Woodhall. "I take it there have been no further attacks?"

"No, but our teams are still dealing with a few problems on *Vengeance*. When are you coming through the portal?"

"We're already moving, sir. The portal is open wide enough to facilitate safe entry, and the Admiralty has confirmed that the next ships to arrive will assume defensive positions on this side of the portal in case the armada gets past us."

"Understood. We should use the little time we have left to create some disincentives for our new friends. I'm thinking a defended perimeter with mines, a co-ordinated torpedo strategy, requisitioning of the giant sphere – the Battle Sphere, as we're calling it – and offensive arrays of fighters."

"Entering the portal now," said Ryan, ignoring Stansfield's suggestions.

"Conway reports a change in the Sphere's activity, sir," said Yau. "No obvious cause."

Stansfield flicked at his data slate, adding Yau to the private channel with Captain Ryan. "Anything to indicate offensive action, Lieutenant?" Stansfield asked.

"Not that I can see, sir," said Yau, frowning at his console, "but we know so little about this thing."

"We're armed and ready," said Captain Ryan, confidence dripping from his voice.

"So was *Colossus*," muttered Stanfield, but Captain Ryan appeared to think his massive state-of-the-art battleship was invincible.

The remnants of the bridge crew watched as *Orion* emerged from the swirling mass of colours that created the portal.

"Amazing," said Stansfield, shaking his head at the sight. *Orion* was new and huge, maybe three times the size of *Vengeance*, with over five thousand crew. "Ryan, what the hell are you doing? Is that a shuttle?"

Stansfield watched in horror as a tiny craft left a bay at the front of the giant ship.

"There's no point wasting any time, sir," said Ryan dismissively. "Your reinforcements are on their way."

"Something's happening, sir," said Yau urgently. "The Battle Sphere, I think it's noticed the shuttle."

"Or it doesn't like *Orion*," said Stansfield, appalled at the implications. "Ryan, abort the troop deployment."

"Negative, Admiral, we're clear to deploy," said Ryan as the rest of *Orion* emerged from the portal.

Stansfield opened his mouth to object as Yau started to say something about engine signatures.

But it was too late. As the shuttle moved out of *Orion*'s shadow, a thick beam of blue light flashed from the Battle Sphere.

The shuttle shuddered briefly; then the beam disappeared. For a moment it looked like the shuttle was unharmed, that it might somehow have escaped.

Then a series of explosions rocked the tiny ship and its panels peeled away, spilling its cargo of Marines into the void.

17

"What the fuck just happened?" said Ten. The Sphere seemed to have finished shifting its parts around, and the structure was now still and silent, but they'd all felt it hum as power had shunted through the systems.

"Everyone okay?" asked Conway. The team all showed green in her HUD, and they called in one by one to confirm. "So what happened?"

"The beam weapon fired," said Davies hoarsely. "Which is bad, 'cos there shouldn't have been anything to shoot at."

"Was it *Orion*?" asked Ten, fearing the worst.

"I don't know," said Davies, a wail of despair in his voice. "I can't see what's going on, the screens here are all off and the doors are locked. I can't get out!"

"Steady, Davies," said Conway in a low, slow voice, "steady. We'll get out of this, and we'll get our answers, okay?"

There was a pause; then Davies said in a calmer voice, "Okay."

"Good, so tell me what we need to do. Take it slow, and break it down into nice, easy steps," said Conway. "Start with the facts and work out from there."

"Okay," repeated Davies. "The beam weapon fired, but we disabled the system on the original Sphere."

Conway nodded inside her helmet. The first Sphere's beam weapon, or at least all the components they'd been able to identify, had been comprehensively shredded by railgun fire. "And your conclusion?"

"Each sphere has a beam weapon," said Davies. "That suggests they're built to the same design, so they probably carry Mechs."

"I knew we hadn't seen the end of these bastards," muttered Jackson.

"What's the next step, Double-D?" said Conway calmly, ignoring Jackson.

"Access. We need to get back into their systems and shut them out."

"Good, Davies, that's good," said Conway. "How do we do that?"

"I don't know!" said Davies, voice rising again. "I lost my kit when we left that last room. I've got nothing left, it's all out there, somewhere!"

"I know," said Conway soothingly, "but the box is wireless, right? Can you connect remotely?"

There was a moment's silence, and then Davies said, "Hah, yes! I'm in! The signal's weak – must be all the steel – but I'm in."

"That's good, Davies, so–"

"Shit," he interrupted, "I left an open link to *Vengeance* while the Sphere was transforming."

"So?"

"If they disabled my firewalls, they could have accessed our systems," said Davies.

"And did they?" said Conway.

"I don't think so," said Davies uncertainly. "Can't tell for sure."

"Then forget about it," said Conway calmly. "Talk me through it, Davies. What's the next task?"

"Hack the system, take control," said Davies.

"Good man," said Conway. "Nothing we can do about what's

happened. Our job is to stop it happening again. You can do that, right, Double-D?"

"Sure," said Davies, sounding back to his old, confident self, "I can do that."

"We're working on your position," said Conway. "We're close, it's just a matter of reaching you. Keep at it, and we'll be with you soon."

"Got it," said Davies. "Out."

Conway opened a channel to Gray, Jackson and Ten. "We need to find Davies and cover his back while he sorts this out. He's our best hope."

"Roger," said Ten. The others nodded. "How do you want to do this?"

"He's in a control room," said Conway. "We know that'll be close to the centre of the Sphere, so we go looking."

Ten hefted his rifle. "Let's make it quick," he said. "I don't trust these bastards not to come after us again."

Davies whistled tunelessly as he worked. He'd already checked the link back to *Vengeance* and confirmed that the firewalls were in place. Now he was sifting through the Sphere's systems, looking for something that would allow him to take control. It was a long slog.

"Lieutenant," he said, opening a channel to Yau, "are you able to help, sir?"

"What do you need, Davies?" said Yau.

"I want to check that you're receiving data from the Sphere over the secure link."

"Confirmed," said Yau.

"And was there anything useful in the files Hunter retrieved? Have they been analysed?"

"We've been busy," said Yau tersely. "The files weren't our top priority."

"Okay, I've got a route in, I think," said Davies. "I'll send you some more files. We need to know where their systems are integrated and where top-level commands are issued."

"And you want to work this out from their files?"

"Yes, sir," said Davies. "I think I have a hack to stop them firing their weapons, but we need to lock out their central command system and replace it with our own in order to control the ship."

"That makes sense," said Yau dubiously. "Do you think it's possible?"

"Absolutely," said Davies with a confidence he didn't really feel. "Just need some time to figure it all out, sir."

"Roger. We'll crunch the files we have and let you know as soon as we have anything," said Yau. "Out."

Davies took a deep breath, paused to check the status of the rest of the team in his HUD, then dived back into the Sphere's computer systems. The hierarchy was logical, but the nomenclature was unfamiliar, and even navigating the system took time. Finding specific features and files when it wasn't even clear that they existed was a non-trivial task.

"Shit," Davies murmured to himself eventually, "how much more of this stuff is there?" He was working via his HUD, using it as an interface to the Sphere's main system and making notes as he went. Teasing his way through the complicated hierarchy of components, backups, redundant failovers and half-hidden decoys was time-consuming and difficult. He was starting to fear that the task might be beyond him.

"Oh," he said with sudden realisation. "That's not a decoy." He opened part of the system he'd previously dismissed and found himself peering into the heart of the machine. "Fascinating," he murmured, copying files and forwarding images to *Vengeance*.

Then there was a hiss, and atmosphere flooded back into the control room. The lights came on, and a few of the dormant consoles awoke from their slumber. In the bright light, the bullet holes around the huge room were suddenly obvious, and Davies frowned as he looked around.

"What the fuck happened here?" he said to himself. It looked like someone had stood on the edge of the room and sprayed it with fire, shredding the screens, the computers and much of the network infrastructure. It was blind luck that Davies had found a functional terminal.

Then there was the gentle swish of a door opening. Davies threw himself behind the console, scrabbling for his rifle as he went.

There was nothing in sight, but on the other side of the doorway Davies could hear stealthy movement.

"Mechs," he muttered, aiming at the door. He opened a channel to the rest of the team. "I've got company."

"You're still in the old control room?" said Conway.

"Yes, and the door just opened."

"That's us," said Conway. "Don't shoot." And she stepped through into the control room, with the rest of the team behind her.

Davies stood up from behind the console and lowered his rifle. "Thought I was in trouble for a moment."

Gray and Jackson waited by the doorway, checking for any sign of movement, while Conway and Ten hurried across the control room.

"Is this your handiwork?" asked Davies, waving at the wrecked equipment.

"Er, yes," said Ten. "Seemed like a good idea at the time."

"I worked around it," said Davies darkly.

"Forget all that," snapped Conway. "Do you have control?"

Davies paused. "Almost," he admitted. Conway just waited, face hidden by her helmet. "No," he said finally, "not yet. I've found the fire control system and taken control, but it's only a matter of time before the Sphere's commander realises what's happened and works around it."

"The 'commander'?" said Ten. "What commander?"

Davies shrugged. "Stands to reason. Something's issuing the orders, probably an AI of some sort, and it must be inside the Battle Sphere now that all five Spheres have merged."

"So we're not safe yet?" said Conway, glancing at the doorway.

"Er, no," said Davies. "But I think we're close."

"How close?" said Ten. "I mean, I'm not one to hide myself away, but it would be good to know if something's about to go badly wrong."

"Because that never happens," muttered Jackson. "Not if there's a chance for things to go spectacularly wrong instead."

"We need to find the central command system," said Davies, "and isolate it from the rest of the ship."

"Isolate it? Won't it be woven throughout the structure?" asked Conway.

"I don't think so," said Davies, shaking his head. "Look, the first Sphere was in the front line, right? The other four weren't backups, they were part of this extended battle group, and that means there has to be a commander, an admiral of some sort, ready to take over."

"Why couldn't it be on a nearby planet?" said Ten.

"Or a sixth Sphere that hasn't shown itself?" said Gray.

"Or with the incoming armada?" suggested Conway.

"It could," said Davies impatiently, "but there's still got to be a local commander for the Battle Sphere, something inside the merged ship that gives the orders. A captain that can operate if the Sphere is alone or cut off from outside contract."

Davies pulled up a 3D schematic he had found of the Battle Sphere and flashed it into the team's HUDs. "I think it's here," he said, dropping a flag into the plan.

"That's not something we saw in the original Sphere," conceded Ten. "Looks like something new."

"Let's say you're right," said Conway. "What's our next step?"

"Something's controlling this ship," insisted Davies. "We need to find it, supplant it, and take control ourselves. If we don't, it's only a matter of time till the death beam fires on *Vengeance* and *Orion*."

"Game over, man," said Jackson with a sad shake of his head, "game over."

Conway was quiet for a moment, thinking it over. "Agreed," she said finally. She opened a channel to *Vengeance* and *Orion* and delivered a brief update. "It's time to bring in the troops, sir."

"Thank you, Corporal," said Stansfield. "You'll have reinforcements as soon as we're able to deliver them."

"Thank you, sir," said Conway.

"I will send a company of Marines under Captain Figgis," said Ryan coldly, his voice dripping with hostility and scepticism. "You will now take your orders from Captain Figgis. *Orion* out."

"Good work, Charlie Team," said Stansfield. "Keep it together and we might still get out of this. *Vengeance* out."

"This day just keeps getting better," muttered Ten when he was sure they had the channel to themselves again.

"You know Figgis?" asked Gray.

Ten hesitated. "I know his reputation," he said, noncommittally.

"And?"

Ten hesitated again, then sighed and shook his head. "Let's just focus on the job at hand," he said wearily.

"At least *Orion* can send shuttles without them being fried by the Sphere," said Conway.

"Or sliced into sushi and incorporated into the fabric of an enemy vessel," said Jackson.

"Oh, shit," said Ten quietly. The others all turned to look at him. "We found *Centurion*'s name plate on the Sphere's inner hull."

"Yes," said Conway. "So what?"

"*Centurion* encounters the Sphere's builders," said Ten slowly, as if piecing together his thoughts as he spoke, "and gets torn apart. Her panels are incorporated into a Sphere, her systems are stripped for knowledge, and the enemy sits back to wait for the next enemy ship to fly through the portal."

"*Colossus*," said Davies.

"Right," agreed Ten. "But she isn't what the Sphere expects to see. The Sphere's waiting for more ships like *Centurion*, so *Colossus* gets fried."

"Okay," said Conway, "but so what?"

"*Centurion* went missing about a century ago, right?" said Ten. "And *Vengeance* has been sitting out here in the dark, waiting for the portal to reappear for, what, about a hundred years?"

"I don't see where you're going with this, Ten," said Conway.

"What else does Stansfield know about this armada?" said Jackson.

"Yeah," said Ten quietly. "So maybe it *was* Commander Vernon, in the study, with the candlestick."

"What?" said Conway.

"You think Stansfield knows more than he's letting on?" said Jackson.

"He's an admiral," pointed out Conway. "Knowing more than he's letting on is part of the job description."

"Yeah," said Ten. "I just hope he's going to share his intel before this alien armada arrives."

"Charlie Team, this is Lieutenant Yau."

"Go ahead, sir," said Davies.

"We've got a problem over here," said Yau.

Davies felt a brick form in his stomach. "Yes?" he asked, not wanting to know the answer.

"We've got an intrusion alert on *Vengeance*, which seems to originate from that connection you set up to the Sphere. Is that possible?" asked Yau.

"Er, I–" Davies began, his mind racing.

Then they heard the familiar clank of feet on steel decking. The Mechs were back.

18

"Admiral, we've found Hunter on Deck Three," said Kearney. "We're moving to engage."

"Very good," said Stansfield. "Keep me informed. Hunter's off switch is armed and ready. I can take him down at a moment's notice. Out."

"You heard that?" asked Kearney, looking first a Mason and then at the team of Marines who still accompanied them.

"Yeah," growled Mason, "we heard."

"I think he's serious," said Kearney, "so let's make sure we don't have to test him."

There was a round of nodding from the eight Marines in the team. Then Kearney went on with her briefing.

"The mission is to engage, disarm and disable, okay? We do *not* want a kill. If you can, take out the OctoBots attached to his head, but not with a bullet. Knives only, stab the brain through the casing."

She looked at each member of the team in turn, checking that they had understood the mission. Hunter had fast become one of the team, and she wasn't about to lose him.

"I want two teams of three to herd him toward that dead end along the third corridor fork," said Kearney.

"And I'll set up a little trap for him," said Mason, "something to take him down nice and neat."

The lights flickered.

"What was that?" said Kearney, looking around.

"Batteries running out," said one of the Marines. Kearney glared at him.

"Okay, let's do this," Mason interjected. "Remember, we want him alive."

The two teams of Marines set off along different sides of the corridor, armed and alert. Hunter was a better friend than he was a foe.

"Have you got this in hand?" asked Kearney.

"Yup. Just make sure you don't miss when it comes to the crunch," said Mason.

Kearney snorted and jogged after the second group of Marines, leaving Mason to head for the dead-end corridor with his bag of tricks.

Mason hummed quietly as he unpacked his explosives and tools. He needed to work fast and smart; there was no time for a test run. As he set about building his trap, he heard shooting along the corridor. "What's happening, Kearney?"

"Bloody OctoBots!" she replied. "Remember that cluster we hadn't cleared out? Some of them came looking for us."

"Any sign of Vernon?"

"No," said Kearney, "but I'm hoping that's what they're protecting. They're up to something with Vernon, fuck knows what. I've had no visual yet – over there, Marine, shoot that OctoBot."

"I'll leave you to it," said Mason, signing off as Kearney shouted her way down the corridor with her team.

"The damn Bots are dropping off the ceilings," Kearney said as she followed her team along the corridor. Most were armoured, but all seemed to be vulnerable to the OctoBots. There was more gunfire from ahead.

"Resist that," said a Marine, smashing an armoured foot onto a crippled OctoBot. The thing went limp, legs twitching briefly before falling still.

"Watch out, Roach," called Kearney. "Don't let them drop on you! If they clamp on your head, that's you a goner!"

Roach turned and nodded, then raised his weapon and shot just above Kearney's head. A splash of brain dropped onto her shoulder.

"Shit," said Kearney, jumping clear and staring up into a vent. Nothing moved in the torchlight, and she moved on. "Thanks," she said with feeling. "Can't believe they're dropping from vents. Oldest trick in the book."

"Easy mistake to make," said Roach with a careless shrug. "And this ain't my first bug hunt."

Kearney filed that away for future investigation, and they hurried after the rest of the team. There were OctoBot corpses everywhere, but so far the Marines seemed to be coming out on top. Of Hunter, there was no sign.

Then the lights went out. There was no backup lighting, and the corridor was completely dark.

"Lieutenant Yau," said Kearney as the Marines' HUD and helmet lamps flicked on, "are you having problems with the lights, sir, or is it just us?"

"Just your level, Kearney. We think it's some sort of malware or virus. Sorry, there's nothing we can do until we flush it out. Fernandez and Davies are working on it now."

"Roger, understood," said Kearney, looking around. The corridor, never very appealing, was a lot less inviting without overhead lighting. "I've done some interesting things in the dark," she muttered, "but hunting bugs wasn't on my bucket list."

"Is that what we're doing?" said Roach, standing closer than Kearney had realised. "I think they're hunting us now."

Then there came the gentle tappity-tap of tiny metal feet on the steel of the deck, walls and ceiling. The Marines' lamps flashed across every surface as they hunted for the source of the noise, but the Bots were all but invisible.

"I can't see shit," she whispered to Roach. "Where the fuck are they?"

"Maybe those encasements shield them?" he suggested.

"Maybe," she said quietly as the team huddled together, unconsciously closing the gaps between them like primitive hunters gathering together around a fire. "We need to clear this corridor and get to Hunter."

Then Kearney screamed as an OctoBot dropped onto her head. It scrabbled at her hair, and she could feel its feet searching for purchase on the top of her skull. She dropped her rifle and grappled with the thing, ripping it away before it could take a solid grip.

"Fuck off," she yelled as she hurled it away. Another tapped at her foot, and she kicked out. Kearney drew her pistol and fired at a shape that flashed through the lamps of her HUD.

Roach fought his own battle at her side. Two of the creatures had clamped onto him, one at the top of his leg, the other at the side of his arm. He was swatting away, and Kearney had to shout to get him to stop.

"Hold still," she said, working the barrel of her pistol under one of the OctoBots. Brains sprayed across the corridor when she pulled the trigger; then Roach stabbed at the other OctoBot and tore it away from his leg.

"Persistent little fuckers," he murmured.

Then, in the darkness, Kearney heard a deathly scream.

"That's the Unborn," she said as she snatched her rifle up and holstered her pistol. "Doesn't sound like it's in intellectual mode."

There was another scream from along the corridor and a deep rolling sound along the deck, like a bowl running along wooden boards. A Marine's head, torn off by the Unborn, came bouncing down the corridor.

She stepped over the disembodied head, then yelped as something stabbed into her leg, just above her ankle.

"You little fucker," she hissed, searching for the OctoBot. Her leg was burning, as if a piece of hot wire had just been thrust through her flesh. She tried to bring her rifle to bear, but her vision was blurring, and she could feel herself losing focus.

"Roach," she slurred, taking an uncertain step backward. The OctoBot followed, taking its time, case glinting as Kearney's lamps played light across its surface.

"Kearney?" said Roach, turning back towards her. His rifle spat and the OctoBot at Kearney's feet shattered.

Kearney raised her hand to wave her thanks, but it all seemed so difficult. Why was she here? The corridor was spinning around her, and the air seemed so cold. And why was it so difficult to speak?

There was a roar; then something passed her in the dark, moving at great speed.

"Thanks, Roach," she muttered. Her voice sounded strange. Roach was silent, but she could still sense him at her side. She turned so that her torchlight shone towards him, and his headless body dropped to the floor.

The Unborn was in the corridor, only a few metres away.

"Mason," she hissed, fighting to form the words. "New plan. I'm leading the Unborn to you."

"Okay," said Mason. "Good job this is an internal corridor, otherwise I might have breached the hull. I'll warn the bridge to secure this section in case there's damage. I'm ready when you are."

Kearney was struggling to stay conscious. Whatever the Bot had injected into her had slowed her down and caused her to lose focus.

Unborn–Mason–trap. She kept repeating the words.

The last two members of her team were dead, their status flags in her HUD turning suddenly red. She was alone, and now she could hear the Unborn searching for her.

She ducked away, trying to lead the thing back towards Mason. She could hear heavy boots making their way up from the far end of the corridor, but that was a separate problem. She waited till she felt the beast's fetid breath against her face, then she dived away, forcing herself out of its path. Whatever venom the OctoBot had injected into her had severely decreased her agility, and she stumbled as she ran.

The monster turned fast, trying to figure out where she'd gone. It screamed and stormed towards her, arms outstretched to scoop her up as it blindly groped along the walls.

Kearney felt like she was going to pass out, but she kept lifting her feet, forcing herself to keep moving. She ducked–more luck than judgement–as the Unborn caught up and swept past her. It charged along the corridor and Kearney staggered after it. Behind her, there still came the tramp of boots, but she couldn't worry about that now.

"Mason," she said, slurring badly, "get ready."

The beast paused, turned, and roared. The light from Kearney's lamps played across its head, but the beast stood motionless in the corridor. It took one tentative step forward; then Kearney, head pounding and vision blurring, dived under its arms and slid along the deck.

She found herself at the intersection of the corridors. Was this the right way? Did she have to turn? Everything was so difficult.

"Mason, help," she managed, the words coming slowly. She struggled to keep her eyes open, but she knew she had to make one last effort. And now she could hear Mason, or someone, giving commentary to the bridge. His words sounded slow, but how could that be?

She shook her head and pushed herself forward as the Unborn screamed and bounded after her.

"Kearney has the creature now," Mason was saying. "Brace for an explosion."

Kearney couldn't work out what was going on. Where was Mason? And those boots. Where was the sound of those boots coming from? She staggered on, even though every part of her wanted to drop and sleep.

"Run," shouted Mason. Kearney looked up to see Mason waving at he, and realised she'd stopped. She took another step, but her feet were so heavy. Ahead of her, Mason pointed his rifle and fired, aiming at something behind her.

Then there was a rumbling roar, and something smacked into her back. She felt herself fly through the air, mouth open in a silent scream. Then she crashed into a wall and tumbled down the corridor, ending up facing back the way she'd come.

"Come one," yelled Mason, lighting up the corridor with flashes from the muzzle of his rifle as he fired. "Come and get me!"

All Kearney could do was watch as the Unborn came ever closer.

"Igniting in three, two, one ... and impact."

A powerful electrical field encased the monster, paralysing it, and then a high tensile net dropped from the ceiling. The Unborn screamed; then a small, shaped charge tore apart the beast's flesh, killing it instantly.

The corridor was suddenly quiet. Only the sound of boots on steel broke the silence.

"It's dead, Admiral," reported Mason, "but there's something else in this corridor."

He paused as a figure stepped out of the darkness. It was Hunter, a single OctoBot clamped around his head and a rifle in each hand.

For a moment the two men stared at each other.

"It's Hunter," hissed Mason, "and he has us cornered."

On the bridge, without a moment's hesitation, Stansfield activated the device in his pocket to detonate the explosive device implanted in Hunter's head.

19

"Is Hunter neutralised?" asked Stansfield.

Lieutenant Yau looked at the Admiral, a horrified expression on his face, stunned that he would even consider using the device on Hunter.

"Stop gawping, Lieutenant," snapped Stansfield. "It's a simple command decision, but not one I take lightly. Either I lose two Marines with no back-up, or a Penal Marine with a substantial catalogue of criminal activity. Whenever it comes to decisions about the welfare of the crew on this ship, I'll make a similar call."

Yau said nothing, returning his attention to the console in front of him. He thanked his lucky stars that he didn't have to make those decisions every hour of every day, but he still disagreed with what the admiral had done. Hunter had been one of them. It had only taken a short time for him to prove his worth.

"Mason, confirm that Hunter is neutralised," Stansfield said again. "Mason?"

But there was no answer. Mason had other things on his mind.

∾

On Deck Three, Hunter was very much still alive. Mason wouldn't have believed that Stansfield would press the button if he hadn't heard his explanation to Lieutenant Yau, but he might as well not have bothered for all the effect it had.

Mason stared as Hunter took another step, coming in close for the kill. It clearly wasn't Hunter who was running the show; it was the OctoBot on his head. Kearney had crumpled to the floor in front of him and looked completely out of it.

"Shit," muttered Mason as he assessed his options. The Bot was the problem, not Hunter, but it didn't appear to have complete control. Hunter's face was a grimace of pain, and his movements were slow and jerky, as if both he and the Bot were struggling for command.

Mason dared not shoot, in case he delivered a head wound to Hunter. If he could get close, he might be able to knife the Bot, but even that was risky.

Kearney stirred, her legs kicking feebly as she struggled to fight whatever it was that had overpowered her. Mason could see that she had clocked Hunter's presence and was aware of what was going on, but she was powerless to act.

"Kearney," he yelled, pulling an injector from a pouch in his armour, "can you stand?"

She didn't answer, which Mason took to be a bad sign. He scurried forward as Hunter raised his rifles. Mason thrust out his arm and stabbed the injector's needle into Kearney's thigh, pumping her full of RapidAdreno.

"Get up," he yelled, pulling Kearney to his feet as Hunter struggled with his OctoBot overlord.

"Wassup?" said Kearney blearily, as Mason pulled her backwards past the intersection and into another corridor as Hunter finally fired.

Rounds tore through the corridor, peppering the walls, the floor and the ceiling, and bouncing around the inside of the ship like balls in a pinball machine.

Mason wrapped his armoured form around Kearney's body,

putting himself between her and Hunter, and yelled at her to wake up. The noise from the two rifles was huge, but in seconds it was over.

"RapidAdreno," said Mason by way of explanation as he released Kearney. She staggered a little, her balance off, but she was upright.

RapidAdreno–also known as Bootneck marching powder–was a battlefield drug designed to give a soldier an immediate performance boost. It was exactly what Kearney needed, and she felt a surge of life as the drug took effect.

"Thanks," she managed. She was awake and functioning, but so, so tired.

Then Hunter appeared around the corner, swinging a rifle like a club. It missed Kearney and smashed into Mason's shoulder, knocking him back across the corridor.

The rifle swung again, crunching into the faceplate of Mason's helmet and snapping his head back. Hunter followed as Mason staggered back, raising his arm a third time, his movements now smooth and fluid as he aimed another blow.

But Kearney yelled and pushed herself forward. Her rifle was gone, lost in the dark. She snatched her knife from its sheath and slashed it across Hunter's calf, opening a deep cut.

Hunter roared in pain and spun around. He raised the rifle, ready to club his attacker back to the floor.

But Kearney's mind was on fire. The RapidAdreno had flooded her system and given her an artificially raised sense of power and strength. Her vision was still blurred, but she spun on the floor, thrusting out her leg to kick Hunter's feet away from him.

Hunter crashed to the ground and landed across Kearney's legs, pinning her so that only her arms were free. He reached out with his cybernetic arm and grabbed her neck.

She felt the cold metal fingers tightening around her throat as she gulped to take a last gasp of air.

And then Mason was there. He wrapped one armoured arm around Hunter's neck and heaved back, while his other hand groped for the OctoBot. The three troopers formed a grotesque diorama, all straining against the others. As Kearney's face began to turn red and her arms scrabbled ineffectually at the hand that choked her, Mason pulled at the OctoBot. The creature's brain pulsated in its transparent casing, its needles deeply implanted into Hunter's skull and spinal column.

"Let go, you little fucker," Mason seethed, pulling at the thing. He could feel Hunter's skin beginning to tear as the feet that held the OctoBot in position dug into his flesh. The needles had pierced the bone, and Mason yelled as he heaved back on Hunter's neck.

But the OctoBot wouldn't come away, and Mason had no intention of harming his fellow trooper if he could possibly help it.

"Hold on," he grunted, tightening his grip on Hunter's neck and moving his free hand to grapple with the cybernetic arm.

Kearney was thrashing at Hunter, trying desperately to remove his hand from her neck, but his grasp was unassailable.

"Knife it," gasped Kearney, "stab the fucker!"

Mason nodded and dragged out his knife. He thrust it at the translucent container that enclosed the brain of the OctoBot.

Hunter released his grasp on Kearney's neck, moving faster than she would have believed possible. Mason's strike was deflected by the cybernetic arm, and his knife glanced across the Bot's case before slicing the skin of Hunter's skull. The translucent container cracked and the sustaining fluid began to trickle out as Hunter roared in sudden pain.

Hunter flinched back, pushing himself away from Kearney and kicking out. His sudden change caught Mason by surprise, and his grip slipped. Hunter heaved back, throwing off Mason. Then he turned and ran off down the corridor, heading off in the direction the Bots had come from.

"Are you okay?" said Mason, pulling himself across the deck to check on Kearney.

"Yeah," she rasped, breath ragged as she heaved in air though her crushed throat. "Shit, that was painful. Did you disable the Bot?"

Mason shook his head. "No. I damaged it, but he's still raging about powered by that thing."

"Help me up," she said, straightening her HUD. "We've got to get him before he goes to ground again."

Kearney stumbled as she moved to get back on her feet, and Mason put out his arm to steady her. "You sure you're okay?"

"I've got this, Mason," she snapped. "Don't give me that look! I'm running on RapidAdreno, I'll be fine."

Mason retrieved his weapon as Kearney searched along the corridor for hers. "Shit," she said after a few moments, "no idea where it went." She took a rifle from a decapitated Marine.

"At least you got the Unborn," Kearney said as they jogged slowly along the corridor. "That bugger was frightening with the lights off."

"It was pretty darn scary with the lights on," said Mason.

"Mason, Kearney, sit-rep," said Stansfield's on the command channel. "Is Hunter neutralised?"

"Negative," Mason replied. He looked at Kearney; she knew what he meant. They were going to collude in a lie. "The Bot must have done something to disable the device."

"They're clever things, Admiral," said Kearney, ready to embellish the untruth. "I guess as they're wired into his brain, they must have headed you off at the pass."

Stansfield could detect bullshit a mile off, and his sensors were on overload right now. "Just get the job done," growled the admiral.

"Roger," said Kearney, muting the channel. "Arsehole," she muttered, but only when she was sure he couldn't hear her.

"OctoBots," shouted Mason, opening fire. Kearney joined him, the image intensifier in her HUD picking out the fast-moving Bots as they ran along walls and across the deck. The narrow corridor was even more claustrophobic in the dark as the beams from Mason's helmet lamps splashed every which way across the surface.

"Above us," warned Kearney, raising her weapon to fire above Mason's head. For a moment they fought back to back, tracking targets that came from all directions. Then, suddenly, there was nothing left to shoot at.

"Any chance of some lights down here?" Mason asked the bridge, panting in the dark as he reloaded his rifle.

"Negative," said Yau. "You're stuck on emergency lighting on that deck. Davies is looking at it now."

"Well, tell him to bloody get on with it," snapped Kearney. "It's not exactly a walk in the park down here, and the emergency lights are pretty fucking dim."

"We're working on it, Trooper," said Yau firmly, emphasising Kearney's rank. "Yau out."

"Two moved over there," said Mason. He fired a burst, then paused to reload while Kearney shot the other.

"Round here," said Kearney. "This is where they were coming from earlier." She stepped over what was left of Roach, hoping he wouldn't have too many bad memories when he was redeployed.

They entered a new corridor. This one was wider, and had warning signs and access restriction notices plastered over the walls.

"Looks like the ship's core area," said Mason as the layout unfolded across his HUD. "Those conduits are where the last Bots seem to have clustered."

"Makes sense," said Kearney. She peered around a doorway. "There are loads of the little eight-legged shits."

"And Commander Vernon," said Mason. In the distance, an unconscious Vernon was being manoeuvred by the Bots into a large access chute that ran across the core. They'd managed to disable the secure grilles that were designed to protect the area, and it looked like they were taking the commander back to their nest.

"We've got to get him out of there," said Mason. He took a step forward and raised his rifle, but something cannoned into him and punched him across the corridor. He slammed against a wall, stunned despite his armour, and slid to the deck.

"Hunter," hissed Kearney as the huge trooper grabbed her once again around the neck and hoisted her off her feet. She swung her rifle around, but Hunter just batted it away with a grunt and lifted her up, slamming her first against the wall and then upwards, trying to smash her head against a low beam.

Mason struggled against the lights that swam before his eyes, chest heaving as he tried to draw breath without throwing up. Hunter was right in front of him, but why was that important?

Then reality snapped back into focus, and Mason saw Hunter trying to brain Kearney by ramming her into a ceiling beam. He was grunting with the effort, sweat soaking his fatigues.

Mason wriggled forward and jammed his fingers as deep as he could into the gash in Hunter's calf as Kearney kicked out, aiming for his stomach.

Hunter reared back and roared, but he didn't let go of Kearney. Instead he swung her around like a doll and slammed her into Mason. Then he reached out with his free hand and flipped the release on the stunned trooper's collar.

Mason flinched as his helmet fell away; then he gurgled as Hunter grabbed him around the neck. He scrabbled at the arm, but Hunter bore down on both him and Kearney, one hand on each of their throats.

Kearney scratched weakly at Hunter's arm, while Mason punched up, trying to deliver a telling blow or catch the Bot.

Hunter was fading, he was sure, but his strength was formidable. Mason pummelled at the Bot as Hunter leaned forward, trying to crush his foes against the deck.

Mason felt liquid splash against his face, and would have retched if he'd been able. He OctoBot's shell was cracked and its liquids were draining away. As Kearney passed out, Mason finally realised that there was only one way out of this. They just had to keep breathing long enough to see the moment arrive.

20

Mason heard his name being called, as if from a long way off. He levered open his eyes and peered blearily around. The world was swimming, his neck ached, and he could barely draw breath.

"Damn it," Hunter was saying, "what the fuck happened?"

The big man was rocking back on his heels and squatting between Mason and the corpse-like Kearney. The Bot's brain, no longer surrounded by enough liquid to keep it alive, had slithered out of the hole in its container and dropped to the deck between Mason's and Kearney's heads.

Still unsure what was going on, Mason watched entranced as Hunter pulled each of the OctoBot's eight needles from his flesh. He tossed the carcass aside and rubbed at his neck.

Mason scrambled to take a breath. His neck was tight and sore, and it felt like there was no room for air to pass into his lungs. Kearney lay still on the floor.

"What happened?" Hunter asked. "Did I do this?" he hissed, looking around.

Mason couldn't speak. He just rolled onto his side and shook Kearney's shoulder.

"Oh, fuck!" said Hunter as a couple of OctoBots pattered through the dimly lit corridor and disappeared into the access conduit where Vernon had been taken.

Kearney gasped and drew in a deep, life-clutching breath, then coughed it all out in ragged hacks. Mason closed his eyes in relief, then flopped onto his back, exhausted.

"The Bots got you," he said to Hunter, "and that was nearly the fucking end of us. Is Kearney okay?"

Hunter leaned over her and nodded. She was breathing and her eyes were flickering, but her neck was swollen and red.

"I'm so bloody sorry, guys," Hunter replied, distraught at what he'd done. "Please tell me I didn't kill anyone? I had no clue what was going on. They get into your brain completely."

"That deserves a bloody medal," said Kearney quietly, her voice a mangled mess. "Nobody should have to live in your head, Hunter."

Mason managed a harsh laugh, then had to cough his lungs up.

"Sorry," Hunter managed again before Mason interrupted him.

"Not your fault," he said with a throaty rasp. "Just pleased we got you out of it alive."

"And that bloody arm, Hunter," Kearney began, raw and rasping. "The frigging thing almost killed me. You need to put a ... a padlock on that thing."

"I'm so sorry, both of you," Hunter reiterated with a shake of his head. "But we need to move. Are you ready to stand?"

Mason nodded, and the three troopers heaved themselves upright, all leaning on each other and as unsteady as newborn calves.

Hunter winced. "What the fuck happened to my leg?" he said, twisting to look. "It hurts like hell."

"You picked up a scratch," said Kearney with a sniff. "Let's just say we're even and leave it at that."

Mason made a sign indicating that the Marines should mute their audio channels. He paused, then said, "Stansfield tried to blow your head off back there."

"Bollocks," said Hunter, not believing it. "Shit, you're serious? And I thought we were friends." There were a few moments of silence while he thought about it. "I'd have done the same," he said at last. "Given the circumstances, I'd have made the same call."

"Such a generous spirit," observed Kearney. "It was still a shitty thing to do."

"Hey, we're alive, aren't we?" Hunter said.

"How come your head didn't go pop?" asked Mason. "Is there something you want to tell us? We spun Stansfield some yarn about the OctoBots suppressing the device."

"No way he believed it," muttered Kearney.

"Maybe, maybe not," said Mason, "but we've got your back, Hunter. If we stick to the story, he'll be none the wiser."

"Promise you can keep a secret?" Hunter asked.

Kearney and Mason nodded.

"I deactivated it while I was sorting out that cluster of OctoBots. It's the first moment I've had to myself since they uncuffed me. Seriously, they had me cuffed from the moment Woodhall's team captured me to the moment I was introduced to you lot. Imagine wiping your arse with cuffed hands. It's not easy, I can tell you."

"And I thought that piece of brain down there was disgusting enough," said Kearney, making a face. "Now you've made me think of something even more gross."

"So he can't blow your head off anymore?" Mason asked.

"Yes and no," said Hunter as he collected a rifle and checked its magazine. "The device is still in my head, but it's been deactivated. It's still there, but it can't receive commands from Stansfield's remote. Stalemate; I'm safe till they realise what I've done, then they'll replace it or something and..." He mimed an explosion.

"We won't tell," Mason reassured him.

"Right," said Kearney. "Stick to the story and we'll all be fine."

"We're clear down here, bridge," said Mason after unmuting the command channel. "And Hunter is back in the land of the living."

"Good," said Stansfield. "What of Commander Vernon?"

"We think the commander is still alive," said Mason, "but the Bots have taken him towards the core. I'd like to send a scout drone along the conduits to find out what they're up to in there."

"Agreed," said Stansfield. "Fernandez, get a drone team to the core and make that happen. Charlie Team, there are medics on their way. I want you patched up and back in action as soon as possible, clear? Mason, I want you to supervise a mine-setting operation to greet the enemy armada when it arrives."

"Roger," said Mason, sliding back down the wall as a team of medics appeared with an escort of Marines in full power armour. "Charlie Team out."

~

On the bridge, attention was focused on the enemy armada.
"Admiral," said Midshipman Pickering, who'd taken Henry's place at the weapons command console, "the armada's battle fleet just jumped again. They're almost at the portal."

"What?" snapped Stansfield. "How did they manage that?"

"Unclear, sir," said Lieutenant Yau. "They must have some kind of jump or acceleration technology."

Stansfield stared for a moment at his science officer, then took a calming breath. "Thank you for your insight, Lieutenant," he said acidly. "Where's Khan?" he said, casting around the bridge for his comms officer.

"Dead, sir," said Yau.

"Dammit," snapped Stansfield, glaring around the bridge. "Hail Captain Ryan," he said, "and patch him through."

"Ay, sir," said Yau, "hailing now."

"Admiral," said Ryan a few seconds later, his face appearing in a corner of the main screen.

"Captain," said Stansfield. "How's the deployment progressing? I take it you've seen that the armada's battle-fleet is almost upon us?"

"Yes, Admiral, we're fully up-to-date. *Resolution* is less than an hour from the portal, so we have back-up close at hand."

"That's good to know," said Stansfield. "And maybe you could confirm what's being sent to us, Captain."

Yau switched the main screen and the approaching armada to a view of the space between the two battleships. *Orion* had moved close to *Vengeance*, and there were over thirty shuttles and cargo haulers making their way between the vessels, each packed with essential supplies, equipment, arms, munitions and crew.

"We're delivering a compete update," said Ryan. "You're getting pilots, bridge crew, Marines and administrative staff. Over eight hundred people in total, as well as food, hydroponics units, cloning equipment, modern water filtration systems, atmospheric processors, fabricators; the lot. *Vengeance* will feel like a new ship by the time we're finished."

"Well, I must thank Mr Woodhall for his excellent work in requisitions," Stansfield replied, completely straight-faced. "And what about fighter craft, Captain? Did the Admiralty send us new stock?"

"Fighters?" scoffed Ryan. "No, Admiral, there are no 'fighters'. *Orion* has a mix of semi-autonomous weapons platforms, fast assault craft and short-range destroyers. Once we've dealt with the enemy force, we'll be happy to oversee your refurb, Admiral."

"I'm not so sure we'll make it that far," Stansfield replied. "We're going to need everything that *Orion* can throw at that armada. We haven't a clue what we're facing."

"I'm going to come over," Ryan continued as if Stansfield hadn't spoken. "I think it's best if you, I and Lieutenant Woodhall meet face-to-face before we engage the enemy."

"Agreed, Captain Ryan," said Stansfield, wondering what fresh idiocy such a visit might herald. "We'll look forward to welcoming you on board."

Ryan signed out and his image vanished. Stansfield took a moment to think it through. New crew and new kit for an admiral who'd been in stasis for half a century. He felt tired, worn out, but he knew that he was pivotal in fighting this enemy. The last enemy he'd fight, if he had his way.

He forced himself to focus on the matter at hand and turned to his science office. "What's going on with the Battle Sphere, Lieutenant?"

"Corporal Conway reports that things are under control, sir.

Orion's crew landed some time ago, along with a company of Marines under a Captain, er, Figgis. They're being briefed by Marine X right now."

"Hah!" said Stansfield. He had no idea who Captain Figgis was, but if he was anything like Ryan, he was bound to enjoy a briefing from the Navy's most annoying Penal Marine. "Put the armada back on the screen."

Stansfield stared at the ships, wondering about the strength of their armour, the skills and training of their crews, their weaponry. Would the Royal Navy be a match for them?

Then the main screen went blank.

Stansfield blinked. Equipment failures were common on *Vengeance*, but the timing couldn't be worse. "What happened, Lieutenant?"

"Checking, sir," said Yau, his hands flying across his console.

Then the proximity alert sirens began to sound, and red lights flashed across the bridge. The screen flickered and suddenly there was just a single ship in view, close up and in magnificent detail.

"Lieutenant?" growled Stansfield.

"The battle-fleet jumped again, sir. They're here, right now. And they're readying their weapons to fire on us."

21

The firefight was fast and heavy. Mechs flooded into the control room, heedless of their own safety, and opened fire as soon as Charlie Team came into sight.

But for all their ferocity and aggression, they were ineffective soldiers. For Conway and her team, the biggest worry was that they'd run out of ammunition before they ran out of enemies.

"This is ridiculous," she said as another squad of Mechs charged their position and were torn apart. "They're going to block the doors with their corpses if this goes on much longer."

The Mechs were now clambering across the corpses of their predecessors as they scrambled into the control room. In places, the pile was already three or four deep, and still they came on.

"How many so far, do you reckon?" said Ten as he reloaded his rifle. They'd settled into a rhythm – two firing, two resting, Davies hacking at the command systems – to conserve ammunition. Jackson and Gray were firing now, while Conway and Ten paused to gather their breath.

"A hundred, maybe?" said Conway. Jackson raised his rifle to signal he was out of ammunition, and Ten smoothly picked up the work, drilling two more Mechs as they attempted to force their way into the room. "Davies, how long till Figgis arrives?"

"Minutes," said Davies distractedly, "no longer. I've opened the main bay doors for his shuttle."

"Let's hope he's brought some friends," said Jackson, "or this'll be the shortest command review ever."

A few minutes later the flood of Mechs suddenly stopped.

"That's Figgis," said Davies. "His company's deployed into the Sphere and they're working their way towards us."

"He can't have drawn all the Mechs, surely," said Conway, peering past her smoking rifle at the huge pile of bodies.

"Time to go, either way," said Ten, moving quickly down the room towards the corpse-crowded doors.

"There'll be more of them out there," warned Jackson. "Hundreds, probably, waiting to ambush us."

"Maybe," said Ten as he picked his way across the bodies, "but there'll be scores of OctoBots in here any minute. You want to hang around to say hello?"

Jackson didn't, and neither did the rest of the team. They followed Ten into the corridor beyond the control room.

"Which way, Davies?" said Conway.

"Stairs," he said, pointing, "and up five flights to the master command room."

"You're sure about this?" said Ten as they climbed the empty stair.

"No," said Davies, "but what choice do we have?"

They followed the stairs, heading to the top of the command stack, but saw no Mechs. There was gunfire, though, from across the Sphere.

"Figgis," said Davies, "they're engaged."

Then a new channel opened in their HUDs and a command icon popped up with new orders.

"We're to hold our position and await reinforcement?" said Ten incredulously, looking around at the rest of the team as they climbed the last run of stairs.

"Fuck that shit," said Conway. "We don't take orders from him."

She braced to one side of the double doors at the top of the stairs and waited for the rest of the team to find their positions.

"On three," she said, counting down with her fingers.

Ten punched the door control on zero and Gray and Jackson slid into the room beyond, rifles raised and ready. Conway and Davies followed, with Ten bringing up the rear. They trooped into the huge room, all searching for something to shoot.

"Where are they all?" asked Conway, suspicious.

"Not here," said Davies as he scuttled over to a console and settled down. "I'm in," he said a moment later. "And yes, this is it. Let's see," he said, chortling to himself as he inspected the system and planned his moves.

Ten drifted across the room to the doors on the far side and triggered the mechanism. They slid silently open to reveal a horde of Mechs approaching at speed. Ten hurriedly closed the doors again and retreated back across the room.

"Company," he said quietly, "and lots of it."

"Positions," said Conway. "We need to buy Davies the time he needs to shut this shit down."

The team scattered, taking cover behind consoles and equipment racks. Only Davies remained where he stood, hunched over the console and working as fast as he could.

"Prep the lock, check the backups, switch out the encryption key," he muttered to himself as he worked. "Almost there," he said, "just a little longer."

They could hear the feet outside the door.

"Steady," said Conway as the door opened. She raised her rifle and flicked off the safety. "Steady."

The doors opened just as Davies said quietly, "*Et voilà!*"

Nothing happened.

The team were silent and immobile, frozen in place as they waited for the Mechs to arrive. After a few seconds, Ten glanced at Davies, who gave a little victory dance.

"What have you done?" Ten asked as he stepped out from around his console and eased towards the doors, rifle raised and ready.

"Mechs disabled, enemy command unit isolated and on restricted power. The ship," said Davies smugly. "is ours."

"Sweet," said Ten, peering carefully around the doorframe. The corridor was filled with Mechs, all standing in neat rows. Ten poked one, and it rocked back on its heels. He pulled the weapon from its unresisting hands and stepped back. "Nice job."

There was a sudden commotion at the far end of the corridor, and Ten eased back, dropping the Mech weapon to raise his rifle.

"Company," he said peering into the gloom.

Then a figure forced its way between the Mechs. A Marine in power armour stepped out from the front row and nodded to Ten. There was a click, and the Marine removed her helmet.

"Wotcha," she said with a grin. "Greetings from *Orion*. Are we late?"

22

"Action stations," ordered Stansfield, as calm as if he'd ordered a cheese sandwich rather than issued a call to battle. "All hands to their posts. Hail *Orion*, Lieutenant. And somebody ask Lieutenant Woodhall if he'd care to join us on the bridge."

"Captain Ryan on your screen now, sir," said Yau.

Ryan was on the shuttle already, making his way over to *Vengeance*.

"You're aware of our situation, Captain?" said Stansfield.

"Yes, sir, I just saw the update. How many battleships?"

"We count six," said Stansfield.

"They're getting ready to fire, sir," said Yau as he covered the weapons console.

"Battle Sphere, this is Stansfield. What's your status?"

"Reading you loud and clear, Admiral," came Ten's voice. Stansfield frowned, annoyed by the Marine's cheery tone. "We have control of the Battle Sphere. Where do you need us?"

There was a small cheer from across the bridge, quickly silenced as Stansfield raised his hand.

"You see that fleet of enemy battleships, Marine X? I'd very much like you to give them a sound thrashing while *Vengeance* completes her fault recovery."

"Understood, sir," said Ten jauntily. "Let me see what we can do."

Stansfield wasn't sure he wanted to know what the Battle Sphere could do. He turned his attention back to *Vengeance*.

"Hunter, I want you and Kearney back in the field. I need you to find Commander Vernon."

"Ay, sir," said Kearney. "We're on it."

"Where's *Resolution*?" demanded Stansfield. "Are we still exposed on the other side of the portal?"

Before anyone could answer, a new group of people arrived on the bridge. All wore current-generation Royal Navy clones in modern uniforms; the relief bridge crew from *Orion*.

"Lieutenant Curtis, sir," said their leader, saluting smartly before Stansfield. "Captain Ryan's compliments, and he offers all assistance."

Stansfield snapped a salute in response and nodded. "We have some vacancies, Lieutenant. If you'd like to take a seat?"

"Thank you, sir, it's an honour." Curtis snapped a command and his team spread out across the bridge, filling the empty spots and quickly reviewing their new positions. Curtis found himself a spot beside Lieutenant Yau, who looked almost pleased to have some company. Stansfield watched for a few seconds, but he couldn't fault their attitude or enthusiasm.

"Welcome aboard," he said as he looked around the bridge. "It's good to have a full team again, and I hope you're ready, because this is not a drill." He was immediately reassured by the sure-handed way the newcomers set about tasks. It was obvious they'd been trained on *Vengeance*'s obsolete controls and technology, and Stansfield had to wonder exactly when that decision had been made. Was it a reaction to the current situation, or part of a larger plan?

There was no time to worry about that now. The bridge might be quiet, but the six enemy ships were manoeuvring into position. They were unfamiliar in shape and construction. There was nothing about them to hint at their allegiance, and it was only their layout and design patterns that suggested they were crewed by humans.

"Let's get things going," said Stansfield. "Open a hailing frequency, Midshipman, er…"

"Campbell, sir," said an unfamiliar face with a light Scottish accent. "From *Orion*. Hailing now, sir. No response."

"Keep trying," said Stansfield. "We need to make contact."

Woodhall walked onto the bridge, bringing with him a faint whiff of furniture polish.

"Good of you to join us, Lieutenant," said Stansfield. "The enemy is before us. What do you recommend?"

Woodhall stared at the ships on the screen, mouth open. He looked like a wraith had paid him a visit and signed him up to the pale, white and ghostly club.

"Orders from the Admiralty are not to engage unless strictly necessary," he blurted. "And to make contact if possible."

"All in hand, Lieutenant. What else?" said Stansfield. He knew it was petty, but the Lieutenant's obvious discomfort was somehow refreshing.

Woodhall boggled at the screen, more obviously out of his depth than any officer Stansfield could remember serving with. "Isn't that ship about to fire?" he murmured.

"The enemy battleship?" said Stansfield. "Probably. You wished to take command, Lieutenant, so what should we do?"

Woodhall watched, frozen by indecision. The atmosphere on the bridge grew more tense as, one by one, every face turned to stare at him.

"We're waiting, Lieutenant," said Stansfield coldly.

"Er, action stations?" said Woodhall, wringing his hands.

"We're already at action stations," said Stansfield calmly, pointing at the status indicators around the bridge. "What action would you and Captain Ryan like me to take next?"

"Er," said Woodhall, dragging his gaze from the screen to look at Curtis.

"Don't look at him" snapped Stansfield, "look at me. Your orders, Lieutenant?"

"Evasive manoeuvres?" said Woodhall hopefully.

"Wrong," shouted Stansfield. "This isn't a training mission, Lieutenant. Stop fucking around and give me an order!"

"I, er, I don't, er," said Woodhall, panicking.

"Incoming," said Midshipman Pickering at the weapons console as the sirens sounded again. "The lead battleship has fired two torpedoes, sir, targeting the last of *Orion*'s shuttles."

"Hurry up, Lieutenant," roared Stansfield. "People are about to die. What are you going to do?"

Woodhall shook as if he'd been slapped, his face so white he might have been dead himself. Then he went slightly green around the eyes and turned quickly away, doubling over as he puked across the deck.

"Escort Lieutenant Woodhall to the medical bay," said Stansfield, waving at a security team. "And target those torpedoes with the forward railgun battery, Miss Pickering. Fire when ready."

"Ay, sir," said Pickering, hands flying across her console as she activated the defensive railgun batteries and targeted the torpedoes. "Firing now." There was a pause; then Pickering delivered her verdict. "Torpedoes neutralised, impact in two hundred and seventy seconds, threat nil."

"Thank you, Miss Pickering," said Stansfield. "Defensive fire as appropriate from now on. What are our offensive options?"

"Unclear, sir," said Pickering with a confused frown. "Nothing seems to be working properly."

"Welcome to *Vengeance*," said Lieutenant Yau. "Torpedo batteries are still offline, sir, and most of our railguns are inactive. Engines are also offline, as is the hyperspace drive."

"Of course they are," said Stansfield, relaxing back into his command chair. Outnumbered, outgunned, and with a ship that was severely damaged and riven by internal dispute, not to mention infested with enemy combatants. At times like this, Stansfield believed it was important to maintain an air of invincible confidence. "Lieutenant Fernandez, how many of *Orion*'s shuttles are safely aboard?"

"Twenty-three, sir, including the cargo haulers. The bays are practically full. The last two shuttles are troop carriers and Captain Ryan's transport."

"Very good. Let me know when Captain Ryan has arrived. Mr Campbell," said Stansfield, switching his attention back to the bridge, "keep hailing those battleships."

"Ay, sir," said Campbell.

"Lieutenant Curtis," said Stansfield, barely pausing to draw breath, "coordinate with the Battle Sphere. I want you to keep on top of whatever it is that Marine X is planning."

"Sir," said Curtis hesitantly. He was frowning, as if he'd heard of Marine X and didn't approve.

Stansfield ignored him and watched on the main screen as the Battle Sphere turned to face the enemy battleships. If there was any doubt that the Sphere was no longer under enemy control, its sudden movement would make things clear.

"Still no acknowledgement from the enemy ships, sir," said Campbell. "It looks like they're not the chatting kind."

Clusters of ships had begun to spill from *Orion*'s bays. Bigger than the Raptors *Vengeance* carried, *Orion*'s ships looked far more formidable.

"Now we'll see," whispered Stansfield.

"Captain Ryan is safely aboard," said Fernandez. "He's on his way to the bridge, sir."

"Thank you, Lieutenant," said Stansfield, not taking his eyes from the screen.

"They're moving, sir," said Pickering. On the main screen, picked out in red and assigned identification numbers, the enemy battleships had begun to accelerate. Five bore down on the Battle Sphere, while the other two tracked *Orion*. The eighth ship was also heading towards *Orion*, but more slowly, as if the outcome of the battle was a foregone conclusion. "Nothing coming towards us, sir."

"Arrogant bastards," murmured Stansfield, although he couldn't fault the disposition of their forces. Any cool-headed assessment would rate *Vengeance* as the least threatening ship in the area, even if it included the shuttles. "How long, Miss Pickering?" he asked.

"Sir?"

Stansfield sighed. Midshipman Henry would have known what he meant. Adjusting to a new crew would take time. "How long till the enemy ships pass *Orion's* position?"

"At their current velocity," said Pickering, drawing out the words to give herself time to complete the calculations, "*Target One* will pass *Orion* in a hundred and thirty seconds. *Target Two* will follow fifteen seconds later. Targets three to six will pass the Battle Sphere at approximately the same time."

Stansfield nodded as *Orion's* fleet spread out and moved to intercept *Target One* and *Target Two*. It looked horribly mismatched, as if a gang of children had been dispatched to tackle a pair of armoured and mounted knights, and there was nothing *Vengeance* could do to help.

"*Target One* is firing," reported Pickering. "Some sort of railgun, as well as missiles." On the main screen, the display shifted to show a tactical overview of the battle, with all ships identified, tagged and colour-coded. "*Target Two* is firing, similar ordnance. *Orion* is returning fire and deploying defensive measures."

"Steady," said Stansfield, as if there was anything they could do but watch.

Explosions appeared on the screen as first ordnance, then ships were struck. *Orion's* autonomous weapons platforms and fleet pounded at *Target One* as it drew close, then switched to *Target Two*. The small volume of space was lit up by explosions as the vessels tore at each other, racing forward and past each other in a blur of light and violence.

"*Target One* has gone dark," said Lieutenant Yau. "Damaged, maybe, and drifting. *Target Two* appears unharmed."

"*Orion* is hit," said Pickering into the silence of the bridge.

"Who is Captain Ryan's second in command?" asked Stansfield.

"Commander Scott, sir," said Pickering.

"On your screen now, sir," said Campbell.

"This is Admiral Stansfield, *Orion*. Do you require assistance?"

"Yes, sir," snapped Scott, frowning back at Stansfield from a bridge where the fire suppression systems were clearly struggling. "Would you care to join the fight?"

"We have our own battle, Commander," said Stansfield.

"We've sustained heavy damage to living quarters and hydroponics bays. Has Captain Ryan reached *Vengeance*?"

"He's on his way to the bridge, Commander. Maintain your barrage and continue to hail the enemy."

"Ay, sir," she answered; then her image shook violently and disappeared.

"Visuals, please, Mr Campbell," said Stansfield.

The image on the main screen shifted focus to show *Orion*. The battleship had taken three more direct hits, and debris and atmosphere could be seen spewing from a hole in her hull.

"She hit a cluster of ordnance left behind by *Target Two*," said Pickering, trying to work out what had happened by reviewing the video from *Vengeance*'s degraded sensor arrays.

"This is taking too long," said Stansfield. "Marine X, how long till you are able to fire?"

"Sorry, sir, we've had a few technical issues," said Conway. "It seems the Mechs are able to operate independently sometimes, and Ten's assisting Captain Figgis. We believe we're on top of the problems, sir, but the targeting systems on this vessel are unusual, and–"

"Enough excuses, Marine," snapped Stansfield.

"Sorry, sir," said Conway. "Firing now."

Stansfield watched as the Battle Sphere's beam weapon fired, the blue light ripping across the void. Then *Target Three* exploded, and suddenly there was hope that this battle might still go their way. Stansfield snarled as he reached out to grasp victory, but maintained the stoic composure of command.

"Good work, Corporal," he said. "Do you have any other tricks?"

"No, sir, but this one never gets old," said Conway as the beam appeared again. It sliced into *Target Four*, splitting the ship along its length.

Stanfield nodded and switched channels. "How are those mines progressing, Fernandez?"

"Mason and his team have deployed in Raptors and will arrive at our perimeter shortly, sir. So far, they don't appear to have been targeted by the enemy."

"Let me know if anything changes," said Stansfield, closing the channel.

"Hunter and Kearney checking in," said a voice. "We're going after Commander Vernon, sir. We'll have him back as soon as possible."

"Thank you, Kearney. Clear the last remaining OctoBots away from the core. And get Ed – get Commander Vernon – out of there."

"Roger," said Kearney before she closed the channel.

"I've drawn a blank on the system infiltration," said Davies suddenly. "The Mechs definitely used our link to inject something into the system, but to what end beyond the obvious, I'm not sure. What symptoms are you seeing, *Vengeance*?"

"Not sure," said Pickering, frowning at her console and flicking through report screens as she tried to work out what was going on. "I can't tell what's been damaged by enemy action, what might have been caused by the intrusion, and what's just old age."

"We're seeing disruption to lighting and environmental controls," said Fernandez, rescuing Pickering. "We're adrift, but the malware has inflicted no damage yet."

"Roger," said Davies. "We'll keep at it from this end."

"Energy banks charged," reported Conway, "firing on *Target Five* in three, two, one."

All eyes turned to *Target Five*, but the familiar blue light failed to appear. The battleship was manoeuvring again, turning away from the Battle Sphere to face towards *Orion*.

"Conway?" said Stansfield. "What's going on?"

The four other remaining enemy battleships were also turning towards *Orion*, and Stansfield felt a terrible fear building in the pit of his stomach. "Conway," he shouted as the enemy battleships fired their engines to close the distance to *Orion*. "Conway!"

"Something's wrong, sir," said Conway, sounding very much as if she was on the edge of panic. "We've lost fire control, and the Mechs are on the move again." The bridge crew could hear firing in the background and shouted commands, as if a full-scale battle were in progress on the Sphere.

And now all the remaining enemy battleships were powering towards *Orion*, firing as they went. Again *Vengeance* could only watch as *Orion*'s fleet and hull were pounded by the enemy bombardment.

The Royal Navy vessels returned fire, filling space with light as they desperately tried to fend off the enemy. The two fleets closed quickly, clawing at each other for sixty seconds or more before their relative velocities carried them apart and out of range.

"Commander Scott, what's your status?" Stansfield asked.

Her face appeared on the display, and it was immediately obvious that *Orion* had taken significant damage to the bridge. Scott looked rattled, as well she might.

"We have multiple hull breaches across a dozen decks or more, sir," she said, rattling off a report, "at least three hundred dead and another five hundred wounded or missing. We've lost engine power and hyperspace capability. Fire suppression is out on several decks, and we've lost internal comms."

There was a sudden blinding flash as something devastatingly explosive struck *Orion*. Scott's image disappeared as the comms channel closed.

"Where are you when I need you, Ed?" Stansfield muttered to himself. The two men were accustomed to fighting side by side, and right now Stansfield felt like he was trying to defend his crew with one arm tied behind his back.

There was momentary stillness as the exchanges ceased.

"Hail the enemy again, Mr Campbell, let's see if there's any life out there."

"Nothing, sir," said Campbell. "We're calling, but nobody's home."

"Put them on the main screen." Stansfield watched as the debris from the destroyed enemy ships moved slowly through the darkness of space. He watched the flares of engines as the remnants of *Orion*'s battle fleet manoeuvred, searching for survivors. The enemy battleships were far away, carried clear of the battle by the speed of their attack.

Captain Ryan stepped onto the bridge, resplendent in a suit of pale grey power armour. He stood with his team, and his mouth dropped open as he saw the images on the main screen. *Orion* hung in space, dark except for occasional gouts of flame.

And now, finally, the sixth enemy ship moved. It crawled serenely towards the stricken *Orion*, not racing in like the other battleships but moving forward carefully, like a predator approaching its kill. The ship moved without haste, closing the distance and slowing to match *Orion's* orientation.

She swam through the last of *Orion's* fleet with no apparent care, swatting them each in turn as if they were mere annoyances. Then she drew to a halt only a handful kilometres from *Orion*, her great engines flaring until the two ships were precisely in sync.

"What the hell?" whispered Ryan, eyes wide.

Then *Target Six* fired a brace of torpedoes. Then another, and another. Each pair struck home, tearing great holes in *Orion* and causing her to develop a slow tumble. A few pods and shuttles flew from the tortured vessel, escaping into space.

"No," hissed Ryan, face white with horror.

Then *Target Six* fired again, and a dozen more torpedoes ripped *Orion's* hull apart. There was a huge explosion, deep in the core of the ship, and the great vessel shuddered.

And *Orion* sat out in the void, a massacred Goliath, her corpse tumbling slowly away as debris and wreckage spilled into space.

There was silence on the bridge of *Vengeance*.

Then Midshipman Pickering spoke. "*Target Two* has turned, sir. She's heading for *Vengeance*."

Stansfield took a deep breath. "Get ready to throw everything we've got at them," he ordered. "They're not indestructible. We just need a little luck, and we'll bag some scalps of our own."

But even before he'd finished issuing his orders, the infection loaded into *Vengeance's* systems activated its payload. The screens went first, then the lights, plunging the ship into darkness. The emergency lighting system flickered on briefly, then failed. Then the whir of the circulation fans stopped, and the artificial gravity failed.

"Shit," said Yau quietly, flicking at his dead controls. "They cut the power. All of it. We're sitting ducks."

23

The bridge of *Vengeance* was silent as all eyes turned to Stansfield. The consoles and screen arrays were dead. The main screen, which kept the bridge crew updated every hour of every day, was blank. The only light came from personal devices and the dim glow of the evacuation lighting system, which was powered by an internal battery system. It would last for twenty hours, providing light for essential maintenance and enough power to stop the ship's nuclear core from going into meltdown.

"*Vengeance* has fallen," muttered Yau.

Stansfield glared at him. "Do we have any comms capacity?" he asked.

"Nothing, Admiral, we're completely dead," said Yau. For a man used to offering solutions, it was an answer he didn't want to give.

"Ideas, please, bridge crew," said Stansfield, horribly aware that he had none of his own.

There was silence. Their ship was crippled and defenceless, there was no hope of back-up or rescue, and the enemy was rapidly returning to finish the job.

"Why haven't they finished us yet?" Stansfield posed the open question, but nobody had an answer.

Ryan and his team were desperately trying to contact the shuttles and pods they'd seen leaving *Orion*, but either they were keeping quiet to avoid detection, or they were already dead.

"I've got Davies on the Battle Sphere, sir," said Yau. "No sound, just a text through my personal comms device. They're still alive."

Stansfield grunted. "Are our internal communicators working?" he asked.

"Affirmative, sir," said Pickering. "Personal devices are battery-powered, and they switch automatically to a peer-to-peer network when the ship's system is down. We have limited short-range internal comms."

"I want to make contact with the Raptor crews and anybody who's left on *Orion* or the Battle Sphere," said Stansfield. "I need a full sit-rep, and if anybody can get me a visual description of what the enemy ships are doing, that would be useful."

The bridge crew set to work. Stansfield floated over to Yau. "What's Davies saying? Anything useful?"

Yau shook his head. "The Battle Sphere's been disabled. They're locked out of the controls, but still have power. Davies is working on a fix for the intrusion, but no news yet."

"And why is the link still open if we have no power?"

"We hopped it via my HUD, sir. It's pretty slow, but we're able to make it work."

"Good. Give Davies anything he needs, but get this ship online."

"We have eyes on the outside," said Pickering. "The Raptor pilots are stuck. If they move, the enemy destroys them."

Stansfield swore under his breath. "Any word on the enemy battleships?"

"Raptor teams report they're slowing, sir. Looks like they're coming alongside us and the remains of *Orion*."

The bridge doors slid slowly apart as they were manually cranked open, and Woodhall floated back onto the bridge.

"Why?" said Stansfield, frowning. "Feel free to speculate." He had his own theory, and if Vernon had been there, he'd have asked his friend to confirm that he wasn't wide of the mark.

Nobody said anything. Then Lieutenant Woodhall, who'd been conferring with Captain Ryan, said, "Captain Ryan and I would like to take a couple of shuttles to *Orion*. There must still be crew alive, we need to begin a salvage operation."

Stansfield frowned, immediately suspicious, but Woodhall's suggestion had merit and the pair of them might even save lives. At the very least, it would occupy them far from *Vengeance*, leaving Stansfield free to navigate the current crisis.

"By all means, gentlemen," said Stansfield gravely. "Lieutenant Fernandez will find you a shuttle and do all that he can to assist."

Ryan looked like a ghost. Stansfield could see that he now carried the burden of guilt that came with the loss of his command. Hundreds, if not thousands, of his crew had perished, and he hadn't even been there when his ship had been destroyed.

The two men floated off the bridge and headed away through the dimly-lit corridors. Stansfield gave them a few seconds, then went straight back to work.

"Can we reach Mason and his team?" he asked. "We need to know what's going on with those mines."

"Not directly, sir," said Campbell, "but the Raptor pilots report they're able to communicate peer-to-peer and pass messages back to *Vengeance*. The range of the external system isn't spectacular, but we can exchange messages, at least."

"Good," said Stansfield. "Get me an update. Mason's team might be the only card we have left to play."

On the Battle Sphere, confusion reigned.

"Somebody forgot to pay the electricity bill," said Jackson.

Captain Figgis and his company had kept the Mechs away from the control room, but without power, their efforts were pointless.

"Are we completely dead?" said Conway. "Is everything down?"

"Looks like it," said Davies. "Sorry, people, show's over."

"Shit," said Conway. "Get it sorted," she said to Davies, "or we'll have some real problems."

"Roger," said Davies, "working on it." He battered at the console and swore at its designers. There was power, but he'd been locked out of all the core systems. At least Lieutenant Yau had confirmed that *Vengeance* was still alive. Whatever else might have happened, at least his mistake with the network links hadn't cost them the battle.

Not yet, at least.

Davies felt sick at the thought that he might have given the Mechs an unbeatable advantage. Then he sniffed. "Pull yourself together," he muttered to himself, "and get the bloody job done."

He sat for a moment longer, listing out the things he knew about the Battle Sphere's systems and command structures. Then he grinned and nodded. "That might do it," he said, thinking through his idea and testing it from every angle he could think of. "That might very well do it."

In the darkness of the Battle Sphere's control room, as his colleagues fought the Mechs for control of the corridors and bays, Davies sat on the floor and went to work, whistling tunelessly.

24

"What a shit time for the fucking lights to go off," said Kearney as her lamps came back on. Then she yelped as the gravity failed as well. "What the fuck?"

"Bridge," said Hunter, "what's going on?" There was no reply. "Bridge?"

Kearney glanced at Hunter as he hung in the near dark. "That's not a good sign," she said.

"General power failure?" asked Hunter as he activated a lamp built into the wrist of his arm. The corridor lit up, a tiny bubble of life in the blackness of the ship. "Does it get any worse?"

"At least we still have something to breathe," said Kearney as she oriented herself in the corridor and caught hold of a monkey bar. The normal sounds of the ship had died away, which meant things were going to deteriorate quickly.

"For now," said Hunter darkly as he fumbled with his weapon.

"Stop whining," said Kearney. "You ready?"

Hunter sighed and nodded. "Yup. It's gonna be tight in there, though. Those bloody Bots love their conduits and shadowy hiding places, don't they? Who's going first?"

"You're the man with the glowing hand," Kearney grinned.

Hunter snorted and swung himself over the vent so that he could peer in. "Looks fun," he murmured as he pulled away the grille and pushed himself inside.

Kearney followed, arms outstretched to pull herself through the vent. "It stinks in here," she said, wrinkling her nose. "You've got Mech brains squished into the treads of your boots. You might want to give them a polish when we complete this next mission."

"I'm not seeing anything but vent," said Hunter. "Do you think the OctoBots know we're here?"

"Yeah, I can't imagine they don't. The plan shows vents big enough to stand in near the core, but they're only accessible through Engineering, and that's not a good place to be right now."

Hunter snorted, dimming his lamps. "We're about there. How do you get a grille off from the inside?"

"You're asking now?" said Kearney, incredulous. "Haven't you got a tool in your wonder-arm?"

Hunter drew himself up to the grille and looked through the slats into the maintenance conduit beyond. "No sign of anything," he said. Then he braced his feet against the walls of the vent and pushed on the grille. It swung gently open. "Here goes nothing."

Hunter pulled himself into the larger maintenance conduit and checked it for movement. Kearney followed, looking grey around the eyes.

"I take it that RapidAdreno has worn off?" Hunter asked. They'd had a busy couple of hours, and there hadn't been time to stop for a proper meal.

"Kind of," Kearney answered. Her voice echoed. This chamber was large enough to stand in, and the walls were marked with engineering notices and arrows pointing the way to the core. "It's still keeping me alert, but I don't feel quite so hyper now."

Hunter nodded. "Good to know. I'm turning the lights up," he said. "It's far too dark in here." The lamp in his wrist brightened to illuminate the entire conduit.

"Nothing this way," said Kearney.

"Onwards to the core, then," said Hunter. It was tricky to navigate the conduit in a tactically sound manner without gravity to anchor them, but at least their rifles were weightless as well.

Kearney stopped and hissed, turning to face back the way they'd come.

"What's up?" asked Hunter, peering back into the distant gloom.

Kearney played her lamps across the walls for a few seconds, then shook her head. "I'm just a bit jittery, I keep thinking I hear tin legs scuttling along the floor. Those Bots get to you in the end. There's nothing quite like the feeling that an evil metallic spider is about to jump you."

"Let's take a beat," suggested Hunter.

Kearney locked her foot against a strut and tried to open a channel to the bridge. Nothing. Then she tried a personal channel directly to Lieutenant Yau.

"Trooper," acknowledged the lieutenant. The signal was weak and flaky, but it was there. "What's your status?"

Kearney gave him a quick rundown of their situation, then asked if he had any news.

"It's still dark, it's still dead, and we're starting to get a bit warm up here."

Kearney nodded to herself. Without the atmosphere recyclers and environmental controls, the ship was going to warm quickly. "Any news from Davies?"

"No," said Yau, "but I can probably patch you into his channel, if you want."

"Thank you, sir," said Kearney. There was a pause; then Davies joined the channel.

"Kearney? How's it going? You anywhere near the core yet?"

"Almost," said Kearney, grinning to hear his voice. "Anything we can do to help while we're here? Hunter is with me."

"He is? Great. Might have a job for you both later. Keep this channel open. The signal's a bit patchy, but I'll give you a shout if I need you."

"I heard all that," said Hunter, raising his arm. "I have the technology."

Kearney nodded. "Break's over," she said, "let's shoot these metal fuckers and rescue Vernon. Then you can get fancy with your tech."

Hunter nodded. "After you," he said, waving her politely ahead of him. Kearney pushed off from the wall and moved down the conduit as the light from Hunter's wrist followed.

She floated around a corner and stopped dead as the beams of her lamps played across the conduit that opened up ahead of them.

"Bots," she said hoarsely. "A shit tonne of them."

Hunter braced himself at the junction and stared. Every surface was covered with OctoBots, all blinking away and staring back at the two Troopers.

"Fuck," whispered Hunter as the OctoBots shifted, like a living wave of metal and glass. "Fall back, Kearney. They'll be all over us."

Kearney pulled herself back along the conduit until she was level with Hunter, eyes fixed on the OctoBots that sat, silent and still, around them.

Then she heard it, the inevitable tapping of metal legs on steel as the OctoBots sought their prey.

"How the fuck did they get so close without us hearing them?" said Hunter. He opened fire, and a moment later Kearney joined him. In seconds, the corridor was filled with a spray of brains and metal parts as the OctoBots were blasted apart.

"There's too many of them," shouted Kearney as she emptied her rifle's magazine. She snatched out a pistol, letting the rifle float by her head, and kept firing.

The sound of gunfire in such a small space was deafening, but the numbers were against them. A wave of Bots moved down the claustrophobic corridor, a deadly swirl of creatures crashing like a wave towards them. Some came along the walls or ceiling, stuck to the steel by their magnetic feet. Others launched themselves through the air, flying directly at the two Troopers.

One by one the Bots were blasted apart until, suddenly, the echoes died away and there was silence once again.

"They've gone," said a bemused Kearney. She reloaded her pistol, then holstered it and reloaded her rifle.

"At least we know where they are," said Hunter, eyeing the conduit with distaste. "I fucking hate working in zero-G," he said.

Kearney grunted and they pushed forward, clearing paths through the OctoBot debris and keeping their eyes peeled for metal legs and needles.

"This is it," said Kearney, poking her rifle towards an opening. "Beyond that is the core."

Immediately above the main hub, encased in layers of protective metalwork and foamcrete, was one of the nuclear fusion cores that powered *Vengeance*. In theory, this was one of the most fortified areas on the ship. It was also the most vulnerable, if you were fighting an enemy like the Bots.

Hunter peered inside and swore quietly. Strapped to the massive circular tech console on the middle of the core was Vernon, a Bot attached to his head, with more all around.

"We can't shoot," said Hunter. "Might crack the core."

"Hey, Davies," said Kearney, "I thought you'd like to know. These critters are all plugged into the core, they're all wired up to it."

"Yeah," said Davies smugly. "I was counting on it. That's how we're going to beat the fuckers."

"Do tell," said Kearney, "because Vernon's down here and we've no idea how to get him out."

"I'll talk you through it," said Davies. "But you'll need to do exactly as I say. Hunter, are you connected to Kearney's comms unit?"

"Of course," Hunter replied.

"Sending you a data package," said Davies. "Store it somewhere safe."

"Okay, that's coming over. What do we do next?" said Hunter.

"I'm gonna need you to transfer the package directly into a Bot," said Davies.

There was a moment's silence. "Say that again," said Hunter with an air of menace, "and use small words."

"You need to transfer the data package to a Bot," said Davies.

Hunter and Kearney exchanged a look. "And what, it's just going to lie there and let me do that?"

"There's a data port behind the second leg on the right-hand side," said Davies patiently. "Flip the Bot over, plug yourself in, and inject the package."

"Fuck, Davies," said Hunter uneasily, looking around at the swarm of Bots that huddled around the core and Commander Vernon, "I don't know about that, mate."

"It's the only plan I've got," snapped Davies, "so unless you've got a better idea, just bloody get on with it!"

Hunter and Kearney exchanged another look. "I'll grab that one," said Kearney finally, pointing at the closest Bot, "and hold it against the wall for you to do your stuff, okay?"

Hunter looked distinctly unimpressed by the whole scheme. "I think I'd prefer to shoot the fuckers and risk blowing up the ship," he muttered. Then he slung his rifle over his shoulder and prepped his arm. "Ready."

"Three, two, one," said Kearney. Then she pushed off the wall forward, getting a last sharp kick from the tail end of the RapidAdreno, and flew across the room.

She spun in mid-air to land feet-first on the core, then grabbed her target Bot. It was connected to the core by a cable, but she pulled at it and it broke away. The Bot scrambled at her, flailing its legs, and around her the other Bots twitched and shuffled, as if uneasy but unwilling – or unable – to act.

Kearney pushed off from the core and crossed back to where Hunter waited, all the time fearing that the Bots would attack. The beast in her hands jerked its legs and groped with its needles, but it couldn't reach her.

"Do your thing," she said, smacking the Bot on the corridor wall and holding it in place, the top of its case held firmly against the steel.

Hunter paused, hand hovering above the Bot, data cable at the ready. The Bot's front legs flailed around, trying to snag something, and Hunter didn't want to end up plugged into an OctoBot again.

"Fuck it," said Hunter. He grabbed a leg with his cybernetic hand and twisted it off. The metal broke with a graunching squeal; then Hunter attacked the next one. The OctoBot thrashed harder than ever, and across the room its fellows began to stir, but at least they now had uncontested access to the beast's belly.

Hunter plugged in his data cable and triggered the download of Davies' package.

"Three, two, one," he said, counting down for Kearney. Then he yanked the cable free, and Kearney tossed the Bot gently towards the core. The thing tumbled across the room, then righted itself when it reached the core. Kearney and Hunter watched as it scuttled awkwardly back to its starting point and plugged itself back in.

"Weird," said Hunter, unslinging his rifle. "I mean, what the fuck?"

"Is it working?" asked Davies.

"No change," said Kearney. "They're just sitting there."

"Let me give it a tickle," said Davies. "So now we—"

"Hold on," said Hunter, "something's happening."

"Yeah," said Kearney, alarmed, "they're all detaching from the core, every single one of them."

"Righhhhttt," said Davies slowly. "Let me just—"

"Oh shit, they're coming for us," said Kearney, unslinging her rifle.

"Hold your fire," said Hunter, as the Bots began to move around the walls. "We can't shoot, we'll wreck the core."

"They're going spare," shouted Kearney. "They're all over the place! Fuck, Davies, what have you done?"

And then a swarm of Bots rolled over them.

25

"Kearney? Hunter? Shite, what's happening down there?" said Davies as he desperately tried to get a response. His HUD seemed to be connected and the channel was open, but he'd had his quota of cock-ups for one day, and he didn't want to be responsible for the deaths of two of his colleagues.

He fed the code into the Battle Sphere control docks while he waited for Kearney and Hunter to respond. This was going to be a three-pronged pincer movement of the technical variety.

"Davies, you there?" Kearney's voice came over the open channel.

"Did it work?" asked Davies, hugely relieved to hear her voice.

"It's a bloody good job it did," said Kearney. "We had the entire swarm crawling all over us, they were going crazy. Then they just stopped. Every single one of them, just like that."

"Thank fuck for that," said Davies, letting out a huge sigh of relief. Then he paused and frowned. "What's that noise in the background? It sounds like jelly squelching."

"That's Hunter knifing Bot brains. He's having way too much fun. How'd you do it, Double-D?"

"Security hole," said Davies, "and a networking flaw. The Bots have a poorly secured, peer-to-peer firmware update service based on an ancient Royal Navy operating system. We installed a virus, it spread through the cohort, then boom."

"A virus," said Hunter, his voice flat. "You killed them with a virus?"

"Yup," said Davies smugly. "Cutting edge exploit, in its day. It erased their firmware, and that left the brains isolated in a jar of goo, unable to link with their own operating system. I knew all this old shit would come in handy someday."

"That's actually pretty neat," said Kearney, with no small degree of admiration in her voice.

"I fixed the malware problem as well," said Davies, enjoying his moment of triumph. "It was calling back to base for instructions," he went on, "so I redirected the calls, scrambled their instructions, and put it to sleep. Partly, at least. It's not a uniform whole, and some parts are independently active."

"We have power on the bridge," said Stansfield. "How's Commander Vernon?"

"Dazed and bruised, sir, but alive," she said. "Hunter's cutting him free from some kind of metallic web right now, we'll have him in a medbay ASAP."

"Good work," said Stansfield.

"Restoring artificial gravity in twenty seconds," said Pickering.

"We have no power to our defences," said Lieutenant Yau. "Davies, are you able to do anything about that?"

"Not from here, sir. I think that's a job for Lieutenant Fernandez," said Davies."

"No access to weapons systems, Admiral," said Fernandez. "But power, comms and tech are at least partly restored."

"Get the enemy ships on the main screen," said Stansfield. "Hail them again."

"Hailing now, sir," said Pickering. "Nothing, Admiral, sorry."

"At least they're not firing at us," said Lieutenant Yau.

"Small consolation," growled Stansfield, "given their complete superiority." He opened the channel to Mason. "Where's my defensive array?"

"Almost done, sir," said Mason. "We've deployed eighty per cent of the mines so far."

Mason's small team had worked hard to deploy the mines and create a three-dimensional defensive array between *Vengeance* and the enemy battleships. As black as the vacuum around them, the mines were only about the size of a loaf of bread, but they packed an AI-driven targeting system, a short-range engine, and enough explosive power to punch through the armoured hull of a starship and devastate anything on the other side.

"Last batch going out now," said Mason as hundreds of the tiny devices were eased out of a pair of Raptors. "We got them from *Orion*. They're almost invisible, but they see everything around them." This was Mason's element, amongst explosives and the devices that delivered them.

Then Pickering's voice broke through the quiet. "*Target Two* is moving," said the Midshipman. "She's heading for *Vengeance*."

26

"Incoming call from *Resolution*, Admiral," said Midshipman Campbell. "They're requesting permission to enter the portal."

Stansfield nodded and brought up the summary of *Resolution* on his HUD. She was a young ship, commissioned only months earlier and not yet battle-tested, having been diverted to *Kingdom 10* before reaching New Bristol. Smaller than *Orion*, she was nearer *Vengeance* in size, even though her abilities were vastly greater than those of Stansfield's ancient vessel.

"By the pricking of my thumbs," Stansfield muttered as he took in *Resolution*'s specifications. "A formidable ship. Thank you, Mr Campbell. Put Captain..."

"Fontana, sir," said Lieutenant Yau.

"Fontana on screen now," the admiral finished.

"Ay, sir," said Campbell; then part of the main display showing the strategic overview was replaced by an image of a standard RN clone in an officer's uniform.

"Welcome, Captain Fontana," said Stansfield. "We have a situation here and could use your help. I'd like *Resolution* to remain on the far side of the portal until we can engineer a more advantageous encounter."

"Negative, Admiral," said Fontana in a clipped accent designed to grate on the ears of everyone who heard it. "The Admiralty has ordered me through the portal to provide immediate back-up and offensive capability."

"I understand that," said Stansfield, his temper firmly under control, "You'll be able to pass through the portal unopposed; I'm merely suggesting that we coordinate our efforts so that–"

"Of course, Admiral," said Fontana smoothly. "That's in line with the last report we received from Lieutenant Woodhall, and we'll be well-positioned to play an active role once we cross the portal."

Stansfield was silent while Fontana spoke, but his face was as cold as stone. "The situation is dire," admitted the admiral, "but blundering in without a thought for the finer tactical points will simply–"

"Thank you, Admiral, but I have my orders," said Fontana primly. "I will liaise with Captain Ryan and report back to the Admiralty, but we will be doing it from your side of the portal. *Resolution* out."

The channel closed, and Fontana's face disappeared from the main display. The bridge of *Vengeance* was silent as the crew waited for Admiral Stansfield's reaction.

"Get me the positions of the enemy ships, please, Miss Pickering," snapped the admiral after a short pause.

"*Target One* is adrift, sir," said Pickering. "She's dark and appears fatally wounded. *Target Two* has turned, and is now stationary relative to the portal. *Target Five* is also stationary, at six thousand metres from the portal and twelve thousand from *Orion*. *Target Six* remains close to *Orion*. It's not clear what she's doing."

"Thank you, Miss Pickering. Link *Resolution* into our tactical feed," said Stansfield. "Let's make sure they at least know what's going on."

"Ay, sir," said Pickering, "working on it now."

"*Resolution* is moving forwards," said Lieutenant Yau. "She'll be through the portal in thirty seconds or less."

The crew could only watch as *Resolution* appeared through the portal. Where *Orion* was huge and bulky, *Resolution* was slim and sleek, although no less deadly. She moved through the portal at low speed and immediately began to deploy autonomous weapons systems.

"Just as *Orion* did," muttered Stansfield, hoping that *Resolution*'s fate would be different, but fearing the worst.

"*Target Five* is moving, sir," said Pickering. Her hands flashed across her console, and the view on the main display changed to show *Target Five* powering towards *Resolution* from above.

"Open a channel to *Resolution*," said Stansfield, leaning forward in his command chair as he watched the drama unfold.

"Negative, sir," said Campbell. "Connection refused."

"Refused?" said Stansfield in evident surprise. "What the hell–"

Then *Target Five* opened fire, and time seemed to slow.

On the Battle Sphere, a lull in the fighting had allowed the Marines to regroup and the members of Charlie Team to survey the wider conflict.

Davies hadn't managed to restore control, but he'd been able to activate the display screens and route feeds from the Sphere's external sensors to create a rudimentary tactical display.

"It's not perfect," he said, "but we'll have an idea of what's going on."

"What's that?" said Conway as a new ship emerged through the portal. She was sitting on the edge of the console, her helmet by her side and her rifle resting across her thighs.

"That's *Resolution*," said Captain Figgis, glancing up at the screen. He and his command team had taken advantage of the pause to confer in the control room and re-organise their defence. "Makes *Vengeance* look like a cargo hauler."

"Hope her captain knows what they're doing," said Conway, "or this is going to be a really short trip."

"Captain Fontana," said Figgis, leaving his lieutenants to pass out the orders and organise his Marines. "New ship, new captain. Her first capital command."

Ten was sitting on the floor, helmet in his lap as he polished the faceplate with a rag. He looked up at the screen and shook his head. "Fontana's an arrogant prick," he said, setting his helmet to one side and checking his pistol. "I pity her crew."

"That's enough, Marine," snapped Captain Figgis. "On your feet and show some respect, or I'll have you on a charge."

Ten holstered his pistol, picked up his rifle and calmly ejected the magazine. Figgis glowered down at him, visibly angered.

"I said–"

"I heard," said Ten, slamming home the magazine. "I just don't care." He stared up at Figgis, blandly disinterested as the rest of the room fell silent, distracted even from the events unfolding outside the portal.

"Name," snapped Figgis, face blotchy and purple as he stared down at Ten and tried to find an indication of his rank on his armour.

"My friends call me Ten, sir, but you can call me Marine X."

"Marine X? A Penal Marine?" said Figgis angrily, taking a step forward.

There was a subtle shift in the atmosphere as Conway pushed herself off the console and took a step forward.

"Stand down, Trooper," snarled Figgis, glaring sideways at Conway.

"Or what, sir?" said Conway wearily, too tired to make an effort but happier by far to stand alongside Ten than Figgis.

The captain opened his mouth, but Davies interrupted from his spot on the floor, where he was still working at the Sphere's systems.

"Contact," he said quietly.

All attention switched to the screens, and the room's occupants watched as one of the enemy battleships opened fire on *Resolution*.

"Now we'll see who's boss," said Figgis confidently as *Resolution* returned fire. The screen flared as the two vessels exchanged fire. Then there was a flash and a third ship flitted across the view, almost too fast to be seen.

"What was that?" snapped Figgis. "Play it back, I want to know what's going on."

"What you see is what you get, sir," said Davies. "We're a bit strapped for equipment."

Not that there was any real doubt as to what was going on. The first of the enemy battleships was still firing, but its engines were dead and *Resolution* would soon be out of range, having delivered an all but fatal blow. There was a series of explosions along the length of the enemy ship and it stopped firing and went dark, disappearing amongst the stars as it tumbled away, broken.

"Ha!" said Figgis triumphantly, and for a moment the room turned optimistic.

Then a blaze of light engulfed *Resolution*, whiting out the displays and forcing everyone to look away. When they looked back, all that was left of *Resolution* was a cloud of radioactive debris.

"Told you," said Ten sadly, "an arrogant prick." He levered himself to his feet, stretched his neck and peered at Captain Figgis. "Break's over," he said as he refitted his helmet, "time to work again." From the corridors beyond the control room, the sound of gunfire drifted in.

Figgis stared angrily at Ten for a few seconds; then he snatched up his own helmet and started shouting orders. The room was suddenly abuzz with activity as the defenders sprang back to their roles, leaving the members of Charlie Team abruptly alone.

"Did you have to do that?" said Conway after Figgis had left. "I mean, could you just not have left things alone?"

Ten shrugged. "Fontana's bad news, and Figgis isn't much better."

"So what now?" said an exasperated Conway.

"Stay alive, wait for Davies to fix things, complete the mission, and go home," said Ten, as if he were describing a simple walk in the park.

"Yeah, about that," said Davies ominously. The others turned to look at him. "I've done everything I can think of, and the best I can do is a stalemate."

"Told you this wouldn't work," said Jackson from along the room, where he was watching for approaching Mechs.

"What do you mean?" said Conway testily, her patience worn thin.

"Some of the core systems are damaged," said Davies. "I can't take control without replacing them, but neither can the Mechs. This ship is, to all intents and purposes, fucked."

"And you can't un-fuck it?" said Ten. "Just want to make sure I've understood."

"Nope," said Davies as he stood up. "I've been battling, the enemy has fought back, and between us we've trashed the hardware and corrupted so much of the system that I'm surprised the lights are still on."

There was a moment's quiet.

"So what now?" asked Gray finally.

Davies picked up his rifle, checked the magazine, then refitted his helmet. "Find bad things," he said carefully, "and shoot them."

"My favourite type of solution," said Ten. "Let's rock and roll."

27

"Damn it," said Stansfield as he stared at the tactical screen on *Vengeance*'s main display. "Is there no speaking sense to these pen-pushers?"

He shook his head as he watched the remains of *Resolution* drifting away; then he opened a new channel. "Stansfield to medbay. What's the latest on Commander Vernon?"

"The commander has discharged himself, sir," said a voice that didn't attempt to hide its disapproval. "He refused my advice and is returning to duty."

"We haven't met yet," said Stansfield.

"Senior Medical Officer Doctor Julius McWhirter," said the voice.

Stansfield thought on it a moment. "Any relation to Angus McWhirter?"

"I'm his son, sir, newly arrived as part of the transfer from *Orion*."

"Welcome aboard, Dr McWhirter. I worked with your father. He was an excellent medic, the best this ship ever had."

"Thank you, sir," said McWhirter.

"We'll talk when this is over, Doctor. Stansfield out."

Vernon walked onto the bridge. He'd changed his uniform, but he still looked bruised, battered and bedraggled. Stansfield could clearly see the red pin-prick marks where the needles had been forced into his head.

"Welcome back, Commander," said Stansfield. "Are you sure you're fit to return so soon?"

"The Doc ran his tests, sir," said Vernon as he lowered himself gingerly into his chair. "My brain has been declared fit for purpose, but my body needs six months' rest. I've taken painkillers, antibiotics and stimulants, so I'm good to go. You know who that is in the medbay, don't you?"

"I do," confirmed Stansfield with a nod. "If he takes after his father, he'll make an excellent addition to the crew. We have new faces on the bridge as well, but introductions will have to wait. *Resolution* has been destroyed." Stansfield outlined the situation as Vernon sat in grim silence.

"I should have stayed with the Mechs," said Vernon quietly.

"We're not done yet," said Stansfield.

"We aren't?" said Vernon, eyebrows raised. "I'm not sure I see a way out of this."

"Sir," said Pickering before Stansfield could reply. "*Target Two* has turned again and is heading this way."

"On screen," barked Stansfield.

The main display flashed and changed as the tactical overview was replaced by an image of *Target Two* powering towards *Vengeance*.

"She's not exactly sprinting," said Vernon with a frown. "How long till she passes by?"

"Three hundred and forty seconds at her current velocity, sir," said Pickering.

"And where, exactly, is the screen of mines?" asked Stansfield.

"On screen now, sir," said Lieutenant Yau. The display updated to show a cloud of the tiny mines, picked out in blue against the darkness of the void. "Closest mines are approximately three thousand metres from *Vengeance*."

"Hmm," said Vernon, frowning at the screen. "It looks very much as if Target Two will have to traverse the minefield to reach us."

"Yes," said Stansfield as a smile tugged at his lips. "Yes, that's exactly how it looks."

"Do you think they'll fall for it?" asked Vernon.

Stansfield shrugged. "Our engines are out, our weapons are offline, our allies destroyed, and our fighters depleted to the point of collapse. At this point, all we can do is wait and hope."

Vernon snorted. "When has hoping ever got us anywhere?"

"There's a first time for everything," muttered Stansfield as the distance counter on the main display counted steadily down and *Target Two* came ever closer. "If this works, drinks are on me."

"Done," said Vernon, "but it'll need to be the Laphroaig. None of that blended rubbish they drink in the crew's mess."

Stansfield snorted. "Then it'll need to be a solid victory," said the admiral. "I've only got one bottle left."

Vernon clapped his hands together, and they settled back to wait. There was nothing more they could do.

"Thirty seconds to impact," said Pickering a little later as *Target Two* crept steadily closer. The bridge was silent except for the background whir of the life support systems.

Pickering counted down the last few seconds. "Three, two, one. Contact," she said. "Two strikes on her bow and another dozen or more on her flanks."

"How long till the first–" began Vernon. Then a mine exploded. "Never mind," he said as the rest of the mines blew in quick succession.

Target Two didn't slow or change direction; it just went dark. A hole in one side of the hull began emitting a fountain of gas, and the ship slowly began to twist as it flew on. She drew steadily closer, passing within a thousand metres of *Vengeance* before sailing off into the darkness.

For several seconds nobody spoke, as they waited for the impact of railgun rounds or missiles. After twenty seconds, Pickering said, "No evidence of offensive fire. *Target Two* destroyed."

There was a brief cheer from around the bridge, and Stansfield sat back in relief.

"That was too close for comfort," he whispered as some of the tension drained away.

"That's the end of the good news, though," said Vernon. Stansfield turned and saw the commander was grinning. "Because it means you have to crack open the Laphroaig."

~

"C aptain Ryan," came Stansfield's unwelcome voice over the command channel, "are you there?"

"Yes, Admiral," said Ryan coldly. He was in no mood to talk. His return to *Orion* with Lieutenant Woodhall and a Marine rescue team had left him angry and in shock, and he felt like doing nothing more taxing than drinking himself into a stupor.

"*Target Two* has been destroyed," reported Stansfield. Ryan grimaced and imagined punching the smug bastard's face.

"Congratulations," he hissed as he imagined Stansfield's frozen corpse floating across the void.

"There's still work to do," said Stansfield, as if Ryan might possibly be unaware. The rescue team had forced entry via an emergency access hatch, and were now hunting through the ship for survivors. The emergency lighting systems were functioning intermittently, giving the giant ship a haunting atmosphere, and the power to the life support systems had failed. They needed to find survivors quickly, and escape before the oxygen ran out.

"What do you want, Admiral?" said Ryan, not bothering to mask his frustration and anger. "This isn't really a good time to talk."

"I'll come straight to the point," said Stansfield.

I wish you would, thought Ryan.

"*Target Six* is lying about a thousand metres from *Orion*," said Stansfield, pushing a package of data to Ryan. The package unfolded in Ryan's HUD to show the orientation of *Orion* and the relative position of *Target Six*. "A sudden broadside might be enough to end this engagement, if you could manage it?"

"A broadside?" said Ryan, tone flat. Was this idiot really asking him to fire on the enemy? Did he not realise the forlorn state of *Orion*? "Sorry, Admiral, that isn't going to be possible. Nothing's working over here, not even the doors."

"Disappointing," said Stansfield, his tone darkening. "Let me know if your situation improves. Stansfield out."

Ryan stared at the wall in disbelief for a few seconds. "You arrogant fucker," he hissed to himself. "This is all your fault. I'll have my revenge," he swore, eyes burning in the darkness. "One way or the other, I will be avenged."

28

"A pity," said Vernon as the channel closed, "but not a surprise." Stansfield grunted. Needling Ryan probably wasn't a good idea, but even admirals can be petty sometimes, and there was always a chance that *Orion* might still have had a few tricks left up her sleeve.

"Give me a full status report on *Resolution*," said Stansfield. "Is there anything left at all?"

"No, sir," said Lieutenant Yau. "She's gone, completely destroyed."

Stansfield nodded slowly, thinking hard.

"The portal has closed, sir," said Yau. "We have no way to communicate with Sol or *Kingdom 10*. We're on our own."

Stansfield was quiet, thinking things through, assessing the options. *Conqueror* was on her way, but until she arrived, *Vengeance* was alone with *Target Six*. Three ships destroyed. The Admiralty couldn't afford this rate of loss, not with the Deathless pressing hard on a different front.

Vernon was visibly shaken. They were seeing destruction on a scale usually reserved for all-out war.

"What are our options, Ed?" asked Stansfield quietly, hoping his friend could produce some miracle that might get them home.

Vernon sighed. "They always taught at the Academy to look at what's available around you. What are your resources? What do you have left?"

Stansfield snorted. "Back to basics, eh? Very well." He ticked off the points on his fingers. "We have *Vengeance*, disabled; *Orion*, almost destroyed; *Colossus* and *Resolution*, completely destroyed; a compromised Battle Sphere; a few Raptors; maybe a few of *Orion*'s support fleet, if they haven't all been destroyed."

Vernon nodded along, looking vaguely sick. "When you put it like that," he said with a helpless shrug.

"We need to crack this malware and purge our systems," said Stansfield. "We do that, we get our guns back and we can deal with our present opposition."

Vernon nodded; it was the only way ahead. "Or try to, at least."

"*Target Six* is manoeuvring," said Yau. "I think she's looking for something to eat."

"What the hell are they doing?" muttered Vernon.

"Doesn't matter," said Stansfield with a shake of his head as he opened another channel. "Davies, we need to fix this malware. How do we do it?"

"The control package is locked down, sir," said Davies, his voice tight with stress. "Sorry, hold on." There was a pause for a few seconds. "Bit of a firefight here. Mechs," said Davies by way of explanation.

"The malware?" said Stansfield.

"Yes, it shouldn't be doing anything new now that we locked out the control routines, so it's just a case of rebooting or rebuilding all the affected computer systems."

"Can you do that?" said Vernon.

"Not from here, sir, no," said Davies. "It'll need to be done from within *Vengeance* by someone with physical access to the machines, and the efforts will need to be coordinated to ensure that there's no back-contamination of cleaned systems."

Stansfield glanced at Yau, who nodded to show that he'd understood. "I agree, sir," said the lieutenant. "Straightforward, but time-consuming."

"Then get on with it," snapped Vernon.

"Sir," said Yau, focussing on his console as he began to plan.

"Stay alive, Davies," said Stansfield. "We're not out of this fight yet."

"Roger," said Davies, "we'll do our best."

Stansfield closed the channel. "Get Fernandez on the case as well, and as many other people as are required. I want this fixed!"

"Sir," said Campbell, "I have Captain Ryan for you."

Stansfield stared at the midshipman for a few seconds until the poor man wilted. "Put him through."

Ryan's avatar appeared on the main screen. "Admiral," he said in a tone that lacked all respect. "We've found a working railgun battery."

"Indeed?" said Stansfield, eyebrows raised.

"*Orion*'s batteries are independently powered," said Ryan, ignoring the admiral's interruption, "and *Target Six* has settled right over the top of it."

"Interesting," said Stansfield. "So you'll be firing at the enemy, I take it?"

"In just a few moments, sir," said Ryan. "Stand by."

Stansfield muted the channel and turned to Vernon. "They've found a working railgun battery," he said needlessly, since the entire bridge had heard the conversation. "What are the odds?"

"We're seeing some activity in *Orion*," said Pickering. "Could be weapons firing, but our sensors aren't all that good."

All eyes turned to the screens, as if *Target Six* was about to shatter and disappear.

"That's unexpected," said Vernon mildly. *Target Six* had shuddered, as if rent by internal explosions. "Maybe they hit something critical?"

The shuddering went on for several more seconds; then the few externally visible lights on *Target Six* went out.

"*Target Six*'s emissions just dropped to almost nothing, sir," said Pickering. "Looks like she's dead."

There was a cheer across the bridge, and Stansfield sat back in his chair, eyes closed. He blew out a long breath, then turned to Vernon.

"I'll take that as a win," said the admiral, "at least for now."

"Agreed, sir," said Vernon. "Now all we have to worry about is the rest of the armada, which arrives in" – he glanced up at the counter, which still ticked steadily down in the corner of the main screen – "a little over forty-four hours. No worries."

"That," said Stansfield with a grin, "is quite literally a problem for another day, my friend."

He stood up and stretched, looking around his battered and blood-stained bridge for the first time in what felt like days.

"For now," he said, "let's just claim it as a victory."

"A victory," agreed Vernon, "but by the very narrowest of margins."

EPILOGUE

Ten smashed his armoured foot onto the neck of the Mech, placed his rifle carefully against the machine's head, and pulled the trigger. The execution was quick and clean, and he'd lost count of how many times he'd done something similar in the last few hours.

"All clear down here," he said, waving his arm at a pair of Marines from Figgis' company who were checking the other end of the corridor. The clean-up was going well, but it was long, slow work, and risky.

Since *Orion*'s surprise resurrection and the destruction of the enemy battleship known as *Target Six*, the Marines had been working their way through the Battle Sphere, eliminating Mechs as they went.

It was a big job. There were hundreds of them, but numbers mattered little in the narrow corridors and confined spaces of the Sphere. The Marines, long experienced in the art of urban warfare, were systematically clearing the Sphere. Another few hours, and the last of the Mechs would be eliminated. And at least the Marines now had working mind-state capture devices and decent comms links, even if they were a bit fragile.

But beyond it all, out there in the void, Ten knew that the real enemy was yet to be fought. The regular pulse that had plagued them ever since they'd come through the portal was still present, even in the Sphere's damaged systems.

They might have won the battle, but the war had yet to begin.

And Ten whistled as he worked, secure in the knowledge that tomorrow would bring new foes.

THANK YOU FOR READING

Thank you for reading Armada Book 2 of By Strength and Guile, set in the Royal Marine Space Commandos universe.

We hope you enjoyed the book and that you're looking forward to the next entry in the series, Armada.

It would help us immensely if you would leave a review on Amazon or Goodreads, or even tell a friend you think would enjoy the series, about the books.

Armada is the second book in the By Strength & Guile series with our new co-author, Paul Teague. Paul is the author of many books, including the popular Secret Bunker & The Grid series.

We think you'll love this trilogy that opens the door into the world of special forces operations in our Royal Marine Space Commandos universe.

Devastation (Book 3) will be available for pre-order soon and will be released on Jan 31st 2020.

Jon Evans & James Evans

SUBSCRIBE AND GET A FREE BOOK

Want to know when the next book is coming and what it's called?

Would you like to hear about how we write the books?

Maybe you'd like the free book, Ten Tales: Journey to the West?

You can get all this and more at imaginarybrother.com/ journeytothewest where you can sign up to the newsletter for our publishing company, Imaginary Brother.

When you join, we'll send you a free copy of Journey to the West, direct to your inbox*.

There will be more short stories about Ten and his many and varied adventures, including more exclusive ones, just for our news-letter readers as a thank you for their support.

Happy reading,

Jon Evans & James Evans

We hope you'll stay on our mailing list but if you choose not to, you can follow us on Facebook or visit our website instead.

imaginarybrother.com

* We use Bookfunnel to send out our free books. It's painless but if you need help, they'll guide you through so you can get reading.

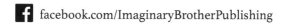 facebook.com/ImaginaryBrotherPublishing

ABOUT THE AUTHORS PAUL TEAGUE

Paul Teague is the author of The Secret Bunker Trilogy, The Grid Trilogy and the standalone sci-fi novel, Phase 6.

He's a former broadcaster and journalist with the BBC but has also worked as a primary school teacher, a disc jockey, a shopkeeper, a waiter and a sales rep.

The Secret Bunker Trilogy was inspired by a family visit to a remarkable, real-life secret bunker at Troywood, Fife, known as 'Scotland's Secret Bunker'.

It paints a picture of a planet in crisis and is a fast-paced story with lots of twists and turns, all told through the voice of Dan Tracy who stumbles into an amazing and hazardous adventure.

The Grid Trilogy takes place in a future world where everything has gone to ruin.

Joe Parsons must fight for survival in the gamified Grid, from which no person has ever escaped with their life.

The standalone novel Phase 6 bridges the worlds of The Secret Bunker and The Grid, revealing what happens between Regeneration and Fall of Justice.

It depicts the world as we know it falling under a dark and sinister force - things will never be the same again.

Paul has been enjoying sci-fi since he was a child, cutting his teeth on Star Trek, Doctor Who, Space 1999, Blake's 7, Logan's Run and every other TV series that featured aliens, space ships and futuristic landscapes.

This collaboration with Jon and James Evans has allowed Paul to unleash his love of space ships and their crews.

He's a lover of Battlestar Galactica, Babylon 5, most iterations of Star Trek and Red Dwarf, and this series of books incorporate influences from all of those franchises and more.

Paul has also written thirteen psychological thrillers, including the best-selling, Don't Tell Meg trilogy and the brand new Morecambe Bay trilogy.

The Secret Bunker website can be found at **thesecretbunker.net**

The Grid website can be found at **thegridtrilogy.com**

You can find out more about Paul's sci-fi and thrillers at **paulteague.net**

Follow Paul on Facebook: **facebook.com/paulteagueauthor**

 facebook.com/paulteagueauthor

ABOUT THE AUTHORS JON EVANS

Jon is a sci-fi author & fantasy author, whose first book, Thieftaker is awaiting its sequel. He lives and works in Cardiff. He has some other projects waiting in the wings, once the RMSC series takes shape.

You can follow Jon's Facebook page where you'll be able to find out more about the first five books of the Royal Marine Space Commandos series.

If you join the mailing list on the website, you'll get updates about how the new books are coming as well as information about new releases and the odd insight into the life of an author.

jonevansbooks.com

f facebook.com/jonevansauthor

a amazon.com/author/jonevansbooks

g goodreads.com/jonevans

BB bookbub.com/authors/jon-evans

instagram.com/jonevansauthor

Printed in Poland
by Amazon Fulfillment
Poland Sp. z o.o., Wrocław

53802468R00120